Rodeo Sweetheart

Betsy St. Amant

HEARTWARMING INSPIRATIONAL ROMANCE

LOVE INSPIRED®
TITLES AVAILABLE
THIS MONTH:

A MOTHER'S GIFT
Arlene James and Kathryn Springer

Sam was up with the dawn the next morning, partially because Ethan's face had teased her dreams all night.

There was nothing worse than tossing and turning against a dream you didn't want to have—make that a nightmare. Who did Ethan Ames think he was, riding into her life as if he belonged there? So what if he was handsome? There wasn't enough room in all of Texas for the size of his ego. Teasing her about her name, as if he should automatically be granted special privileges, was the last straw in Sam's bale of tolerance. If money meant instant ego, Sam was glad she hovered closer to the poor side of the spectrum.

Although poor wasn't going to bring back her father's legacy and hard work.

Sam dressed quickly in jeans and a button-down, then grabbed her cowboy hat. Right now she had a trail ride to lead, a handsome man to ignore and a farm to save.

Books by Betsy St. Amant

Love Inspired

Return to Love
A Valentine's Wish
Rodeo Sweetheart

BETSY ST. AMANT

loves polka-dot shoes, chocolate and sharing the good news of God's grace through her novels. She has a bachelor's degree in Christian communications from Louisiana Baptist University and is actively pursuing a career in inspirational writing. Betsy resides in northern Louisiana with her husband and daughter and enjoys reading, kickboxing and spending quality time with her family.

Rodeo Sweetheart
Betsy St. Amant

Published by Steeple Hill Books™

STEEPLE HILL BOOKS

Recycling programs for this product may not exist in your area.

ISBN-13: 978-0-373-87593-1

RODEO SWEETHEART

This edition published by arrangement with Steeple Hill Books.

www.SteepleHill.com

Printed in U.S.A.

Fear not, for I am with you; be not dismayed,
for I am your God. I will strengthen you, yes,
I will help you, I will uphold you with my
righteous right hand.

—*Isaiah* 41:10

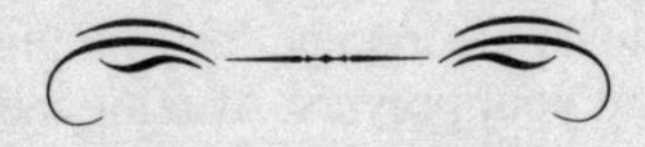

To Cindy—for your strength and your fight.
We love you. Never give up!

Acknowledgments

As always, I couldn't have done this novel alone, especially with the timing I found myself in. I'd like to thank Lori and Georgiana, for your quick crits, your friendship and your prayers. Also my mom, for giving me that one day of baby-free writing a week that really does make a difference. Thanks to my amazing editor Emily for your fresh insight, and to my sweet agent Tamela, for backing me 100 percent. And an extra-special thanks to my husband, Brandon—every day I realize how much of a hero you truly are. I love you.

Chapter One

If wishes were horses, the Jenson family breeding farm would be full of stud mares and furry new foals—not teeming with greenhorn tourists in stiff new jeans and shiny cowboy boots.

Samantha Jenson loosened the lead rope in her hand, allowing Diego another couple inches of leverage. The hot Texas sun glinted off the gelding's chestnut hindquarters, and she swiped at the sweat on her forehead with her free hand. It looked as if this weekend would be another scorcher.

She clucked to the gelding as she studied his limber gait. "Just another lap or two." Diego's ankle injury was slowly healing. A few more days of exercise in the training pen and he'd be ready to hit the trail—though probably just to be manhandled by another wannabe cowboy.

Sam's lips pressed into a hard line and she drew in the rope, slowing Diego's willing pace to a walk. "Good boy." It wasn't the gelding's fault he'd fallen a few weeks ago. Thanks to a careless rider who'd ignored the rules of the trail, Diego had been pushed too hard over uneven ground and tripped in a hole. It was by the grace of God he had only sprained his ankle, rather than broken it. Of course, the tourist hadn't even been bruised—didn't seem very fair.

Sam pulled the rope in closer until Diego's gait slowed to a stop. That probably wasn't the most Christian attitude to have, but it was hard to feel differently in the circumstances. At least God was looking out for her and her mother with the little things if not for the bigger things Sam would prefer. Avoiding a vet bill was nice, but it wasn't going to help bring back her father's dream.

Sam met the horse in the middle of the paddock and patted his sweaty muzzle, drawing a deep breath to combat her stress. No, nothing other than a big wad of cash would bring back the Jensons' successful breeding farm. She and her mother had turned the farm into a dude ranch to earn income, but to Sam, the problems that came with it weren't any better than avoiding the debt collectors. Sure, the new dude ranch business paid the mortgage and had kept the farm from going completely under last winter—and Sam would grudgingly admit running a dude ranch was better than being homeless—but Angie Jenson wasn't the one dealing firsthand with all the tourists. That job fell to Sam, as did filling all the proverbial holes that tourists left in their unruly wake—like horses with sprained ankles.

Sam gathered the lead rope around her wrist and trudged toward the barn, Diego ambling behind. To her left, green hills stretched in gentle waves, trimmed by rows of wooden fences. The staff's guesthouses to her right had been converted into cabins for the vacationers, tucked in neat rows like houses on a Monopoly board. One didn't have to look close to notice the chipped trim, peeling shutters and threadbare welcome mats. Angie was counting on her customers being so mesmerized with the horses that they wouldn't care about the less than pristine living quarters. Talk about pipe dreams. Her mom had suggested selling the ranch several months back, but after seeing Sam's reaction, she hadn't brought it up again. How could they sell? It was all they had left of Sam's dad.

Things sure had changed. Once upon a time, when Wade Jenson was still alive, one would be hard-pressed to find a single repair waiting on the farm. The grounds stayed kept, the paint stayed fresh and the ranch resembled exactly what it was—a respectable, sought-after breeding farm that had been in the Jenson family for three generations.

In a paddock nearby, Piper whinnied hello at Sam and Diego—or maybe it was a cry for help. Sam tipped her cowboy hat at the paint horse as she passed. "I'm working on it, Piper. I'll get things back to normal for us one day." She fought the words *I promise* that hovered on her tongue, afraid to speak them lest she end up like her father—a liar. Promises from Wade Jenson hadn't stopped the bull's thrashing hooves or the heart monitor from beeping a final, high-pitched tone, and they wouldn't make Sam's dreams come true, either.

She dodged a young boy kicking a soccer ball across the yard and narrowed her eyes at the kid's father, who stood nearby talking to Sam's mother. The man was so enamored by Angie he apparently didn't notice the glittering diamond ring still on her finger—or his son wreaking havoc. The ball slipped under the last rung of the wooden fence containing Piper and several mares, and Sam made a dive before the boy could do the same. At least the ball hadn't gone into the adjacent paddock, where several stallions left over from the breeding-farm business grazed. Gelding and mares were much more docile in comparison.

"Whoa there, partner. What's your name?" Sam caught the kid's belt loops just in time.

"Davy." He struggled against her grip.

Sam couldn't help but smile at the freckle-faced kid. A toy water gun stuck in the waistband of his jeans and dirt smeared across his sunburned forehead. How many times as a child had she probably looked the same, playing in the yard between chores? Her anger cooled like a hot branding iron dunked in water and she ruffled the boy's already mussed hair. "You can't go in the paddock with the horses, Davy. They might step on you."

Davy crossed his arms and glared a challenge at her. "My ball went in and they're not stepping on it."

Sam's grin faded at the sarcastic logic. "Park it. I'll get it for you." She shot him a warning look before she easily scaled the fence and jogged toward the black-and-white ball. She rolled it to him and hopped back over into the yard. Davy scooped up the ball and took off without even a thank you.

Sam's annoyance doubled as she led Diego into the cool shadows of the barn, the familiar scent of hay and leather doing little to ease her aggravation. She secured the gelding and forked over a fresh bale of hay, then yanked a halter from its peg and headed for Wildfire's stall. If this was still an operating breeding ranch, there wouldn't be little terrors running around scaring the horses while their dads flirted with her mother. Sam's father died only two years ago, and this was the way they honored his memory? By catering to city greenhorns and risking the welfare of their livestock? Tears pricked her eyelids, and Sam roughly brushed away the moisture. *Cowgirls don't cry,* her dad always said. *They get back on the horse and keep riding.*

But Sam's dad never told her what to do when he wasn't there to give her a leg up.

A horn honked from the parking lot near the barn, and

Wildfire startled, kicking the stall door with his foreleg. "Easy, boy." Sam soothed him with a gentle touch on his muzzle before peering through the barn window.

An expensive luxury sedan was parked near the first guest cabin, its shiny rims catching the July sun and nearly blinding Sam with the glare. The windows were tinted so she couldn't see inside, but it had to be the Ames family. They were scheduled to arrive within the hour, and Angie had already cautioned Sam on being extra attentive to the wealthy guests. Apparently this family owned a multi-million dollar corporation of some kind in New York. How they ended up in the nowhere little town of Appleback, Texas, remained a mystery to Sam. But VIPs were VIPs.

"They're staying three solid weeks, and if they tip like they should," Angie had said earlier that morning, "we'll be able to make all of our bills and have money left over for the first time in ages." Her eyes had shone with such excitement at the prospect Sam almost didn't notice the heavy bags underneath them or the frown lines marring the skin by Angie's lips. But Sam had noticed, and it was the only thing that kept her from protesting. That, and the prospect of having to waitress again to make the house payments. Those exhausting months last year were definitely not ones she wanted to relive.

The doors of the car opened and a well-dressed couple in their early fifties exited the vehicle. The lady smoothed the front of her white pantsuit as she cast a gaze over the horses in the pasture. The car's trunk popped open, and the man emerging from the driver's seat shaded his eyes with one hand as he looked around—probably searching for a valet or bellhop.

Great. One more chore for Sam to pull off—like acting as full-time stable hand, groom and trail guide wasn't enough to keep her busy. She considered hiding in the hayloft like she did that time she was ten and failed her math test. But avoiding reality didn't work—she should know. She'd been trying that for two years now.

"Guess it's now or never." Sam slipped the halter back on its peg, and Wildfire snorted his disappointment. "I'll be back for you in a minute." She looked out the window again to see if the couple had managed to grab their own luggage, just in time to see a silver convertible squeal to a stop beside the sedan. A dust cloud formed around the tires, causing the woman to take several steps backward and cough.

The driver's side door of the sports car opened and a guy in his mid-twenties slid out. He surveyed the ranch over lowered sunglasses, his expression shadowed.

Wildfire ducked his head and blew through his nose, pawing at the stall floor. Sam rubbed the white splash of hair on the gelding's forehead, a frown pulling her brows together. "I know exactly how you feel."

Ethan Ames never thought he'd see the day where his mother teetered in high heels on dirt-packed ground—on purpose. Then again, he never thought he'd see the day he joined his family on a rural working vacation, either. He shouldn't have taken that back-roads exit off the interstate. Nothing was stopping him from speeding farther west and finding some real fun in Vegas—nothing more than his mother's disappointment, anyway. Or his father's incessant phone calls and threats. On second thought, Vegas wouldn't be much fun without an expense account—and his father knew how to hit Ethan where it hurt.

One would definitely have to pay Ethan a bundle to get him to admit that deep down, he was a little curious about this country life thing, after all. He shut the door to the convertible and pulled his duffel bag from the backseat. At least the rental company had given him something decent to drive this time.

"You really shouldn't speed like that, Ethan." Vickie Ames touched her hair, as if the motion could protect it from the country air.

The passenger door slammed, saving Ethan from answering. His cousin Daniel slid over the hood and landed beside Vickie. He looped an arm around her shoulders. "Don't worry, Aunt Vickie. Ethan never passed ninety-five miles an hour." He winked and slung one booted foot over the other.

Ethan rolled his eyes. Leave it to Daniel to blend in with new surroundings like a chameleon. He'd picked up those stupid cowboy boots before they'd even left New York and propped them up on the dashboard for the entire drive from the airport. Ethan didn't think real cowboys would splurge on designer tooled leather like that for a three-week vacation. And what was with that *Dukes of Hazzard* move he just pulled on the car hood? Ethan snorted.

His father, Jeffrey, cleared his throat. "If you two would quit clowning around and find the valet, we could get settled a lot sooner."

Ethan shouldered his duffel. "I don't think this place has staff like that."

"The boys will get the bags." Vickie shot Ethan a pointed glance that clearly said to get busy.

Jeffrey looked around, the permanent frown between his bushy brows tightening even further. "This place is more rundown than I thought. We should get it for a song." His lips stretched into a line. "It better be worth this charade."

"It will be." Vickie gestured around them, her red manicured nails startling against her white suit. She looked as out of place as a bull in Saks Fifth Avenue, just smaller and better dressed. "You know we just need to find a reason to get the owner to sell to us for cheap—before she gets wind of the highway relocation. You said yourself this would be the perfect place for a mall after they move the interstate. So quit complaining—a dump is exactly what we're looking for."

Ethan shook his head. Only his mother could get away with telling Jeffrey what to do. If he or his cousin had tried that, well, it wouldn't have been pretty.

Jeffrey's face purpled. "I still don't see why we all had to come down here to the middle of nowhere and cut a work week short. We could have just sent the boys to make the offer—"

"It's about appearances," Vickie hissed under her breath. "You know the owner is hesitant to sell in the first place. She doesn't even want her daughter to know why we're here. She wants to feel like the person who buys it will take good care of it. You think she'd be more willing to warm up and accept an offer from two businessmen in suits, or to a vacationing family of four? She'll never believe that we want to keep the place as a ranch if we make an offer from New York."

Jeffrey's lips disappeared beneath his mustache. He looked as if he wanted to argue, but wasn't sure what to say.

"Uncle Jeffrey, we'll handle the bags. No problem." Daniel grabbed the largest of the suitcases from the trunk and hefted it to the ground. "Where to?"

Ethan took a second bag, trying not to snicker at Daniel's obvious attempt at kissing up to his father.

"I think check-in is inside there." Vickie pointed to a two-story farmhouse with a wraparound porch. Paint peeled near the faded trim and the stairs leading to the front door looked saggy, as if they'd held up one person too many over the years. "They'll have our cabin numbers. I requested the two biggest ones they had."

Ethan's mouth twitched as he studied the crumpling architecture of the house. "After you, Daniel." He wasn't about to stand on that top porch step with a suitcase. He was likely to go straight through to the grass.

"I'll check us in." Vickie brushed them aside. "You boys get the rest of our luggage." She lightly scaled the steps and disappeared inside the run-down building, an unspoken warning floating in her perfumed wake. *Don't upset your father.*

Ethan grabbed another bag and passed the next to Daniel. Jeffrey stood by with his hands in his pockets, letting others do the work. The familiar claws of resentment dug once again into Ethan's back, and he set his father's suitcase in the dirt a little harder than necessary.

"Watch it, boy." Jeffrey didn't even bother with a glance in Ethan's direction, just kept staring out across the fields spotted with wildflowers. "There are breakables in there."

Ethan bit the retort on his lips and set his father's suitcase upright. Three weeks of this? He must be crazy. No, his mother must be crazy to insist they come. She'd played it up as a huge business opportunity, a real working vacation—heavy on the vacation. But so far, the Jenson ranch was nothing to get excited about. Who cared if the family had been here for three generations? That didn't make the property a steal—it'd just make it even more expensive to buy because of the owner's hesitation to sell, especially if she heard of Jeffrey's plan to develop a mall on site. Families didn't like getting rid of memories.

Normal families didn't, anyway. The only thing sentimental to Jeffrey Ames was his collection of gold money clips. Maybe Ethan and Daniel should go ahead and hightail it to Vegas after all.

Ethan turned his back to his father and shot a grin toward

his cousin, the same easy, cover-up smile he'd spent years perfecting. Jeffrey would never know how badly he got to Ethan, and neither would anyone else if he could help it. Ethan had buried so many emotions over the years, what was a few more? He lowered his voice. "I don't know about you, man, but I could go for a little fun instead of playing this charade. You want to get out of here?"

Daniel sat on the top of his suitcase and rocked back, balancing on his heels. A gleam sparked his eyes. "You know I'm up for anything. Just say the word. Where do you want to go?"

Ethan started to answer, and then stopped as a woman about his age stepped out of the shadows of the giant red barn and headed in their direction. Underneath a tan cowboy hat, her light brown hair was streaked with natural blond highlights, not the fake stuff his mother used every six weeks. Her slim jeans were peppered with dirt and her boots clomped across the dirt-packed earth as she strode confidently in their direction.

A slow grin spread across Ethan's lips. "Who said anything about leaving?"

Chapter Two

"Welcome to Jenson Farms." Sam greeted the guests with a smile, trying not to cringe at the amount of luggage surrounding the three men. Wasn't the family only here for a few weeks? "I'll be happy to show you to your suites."

The older man sized her up with a quick nod. "Jeffrey Ames."

Sam shook his offered hand. "I'm sorry for the delay in coming out. I had business to tend to in the barn." She started to add they were short-handed, but thought better of it. Her mother had warned her not to say anything that would make these guests think the Jenson ranch was less than top-notch—although it wouldn't take more than a cursory glance to determine that particular truth.

"Not a problem." He gestured for Sam to lead the way. She hefted a bag on her shoulder and turned toward the two adjoining VIP suites. They were really nothing more than two small wooden cabins joined with a narrow porch, but these particular cabins had full kitchens, unlike the partials in the other guesthouses. Good thing her mother had added those big garden tubs in the bathrooms last summer, or the Ameses might make a dash for civilization. Why was such a wealthy family on vacation in the nowhere town of Appleback, anyway? If Sam had money, she'd vacation in Europe. Or some deserted island in the middle of the ocean where she could ride bareback in the sand and sip fruity drinks with umbrellas.

"Dad!" The sharp voice sounded seconds before the duffel bag was tugged from Sam's grasp. She turned to find the young sports car driver holding the luggage and scowling at Mr. Ames. "She doesn't need to carry our luggage."

"We can get it." The passenger from the convertible winked at Sam and she quickly looked away from the leer in his eyes.

"Nonsense. It's her job." Mr. Ames turned back to Sam. "I'll make sure you're compensated for it." He motioned her along with a wave of his hand.

Sam's stomach clenched at the flippant dismissal. She'd never been talked to like the hired help before, although with the Jensons' new business venture into the tourist world, that's exactly what she was. Her father's image flashed in her mind, and Sam forced tidbits of pride down her throat. Without money, she'd never get the ranch back the way it was, and the Ames had it to spare. Time to work. She picked up another suitcase, this one heavier than the first.

"Here, let me." The son's warm voice and sudden nearness filled Sam's senses. "I'm Ethan Ames. And this is my cousin, Daniel."

"Sam Jenson." She set the bag down and shook Ethan's hand, noting its smoothness. The men in Appleback all had work-worn hands, calloused from hard work. This guy must not be used to handling anything other than a leather steering wheel or computer keyboard.

"You don't look like a Sam to me." Ethan's dark hair, short and spiky, heightened the deep brown of his eyes. If it wasn't for the fact that he was a dreaded tourist, she might actually find him attractive. He was taller than Daniel, and didn't seem to have an agenda in his eyes like Daniel did, either. More maturity lurked in Ethan's gaze, along with a heaviness that suggested secrets. Maybe there was something substantial to this greenhorn after all.

"It's really Samantha." She allowed Ethan to take the suitcase handle from her. "But I go by Sam." No one but her father had called her Samantha, and if she had her way, no one ever would again. Some rights were reserved for the dead.

"Samantha." Ethan's smile turned slightly flirty, heightening Sam's first impression when he'd arrived in his convertible. "I think I'll call you that instead. You don't mind, right?"

The respect he'd earned by helping her with the bags faded into oblivion, and Sam flashed her own smile as she hoisted another duffel bag in her arms. "Only if you like boot prints on your back."

Sam strode past the men toward the cabins, ignoring Daniel's burst of laughter. She kept her head high and refused to give them the dignity of a backward glance.

"You really said that?" Sam's best friend Kate Stephens laughed, leaning forward to momentarily rest her head on the top rail of the fence. Her curly red hair gleamed in the setting July sun. "Only you, Sam."

"He had it coming." Sam stuck a strand of hay in her mouth and chewed as she looked out over the pasture, unable to hide her smile. "I wish I could have seen his face."

"Priceless, I'm sure." Kate cupped her hands and motioned as if reading a headline. "Preppy City Boy Told Off by Overworked Cowgirl."

Sam shoved Kate's arm down. "It wasn't that big of a

deal." Though Ethan had yet to emerge from his cabin, and the incident happened hours ago.

"I better get back home. It's feeding time." Kate dug her booted foot off the lowest rung of the fence and stretched. "For me *and* the horses."

"I hear that." Sam tossed the piece of hay on the ground. "I'm glad Mom finally found another cook for the guests. Mom can make breakfast food all right, but dinner is another story." Sam and her father used to joke about cornbread that could be used as horseshoes and chili that would keep a body in the restroom for a month of Sundays. She squinted against the memories, determined not to cry. Not again, not today. She swallowed.

"Oh, I almost forgot!" Kate clapped her hand on the fence. "I came over here to tell you something important, and you distracted me with your story of charming guest hospitality." Her green eyes sparkled with amusement. "Guess which horse my father is selling now?"

"Viper?" The mustang gelding was the oldest horse still living at the Stephenses' busy racing stables down the road from the Jensons'. Kate's father, Andrew Stephens, was known for his champion racehorses in southern Texas. Last year, Kate had bought a few acres and a small farmhouse not too far from her family and Sam's, where she ran a successful boarding and grooming service for animals. Despite her own proverbial plate staying so full, she still occasionally helped out with the inner workings of her family's business.

Kate shook her head at Sam's guess. "Think black stallion."

Sam's breath caught in her throat. "No way. Noble Star?"

Kate's red curls bounced as she nodded. "He called me this morning to tell me he's decided to retire him. Dad said he'd rather sell Noble and obtain the cash upfront then try to breed for money later. He and Mom don't have the time for new ventures right now." Kate grinned. "I know you've been waiting for something like this."

More like praying for it every night. If Sam could buy the sought-after ex-racehorse, he would be just the ticket to bring back the Jenson breeding farm. Mares for miles around would be brought in to get a shot at those champion bloodlines. Their business would soar and things could finally go back to the way they used to be—as normal as they could be without Wade Jenson, anyway.

Sam's mind raced in a blur of tallying numbers, and the end result brought a sharp jolt of reality. Her shoulders tensed. She could empty her meager savings and still not have enough to buy the blanket off Noble Star's back.

Kate pulled her keys from her jeans pocket. "I just wanted you to know before Dad started advertising. He's going to spread the word this week."

"Price?" Sam closed her eyes for the verbal assault.

The number Kate named was pretty reasonable, considering Noble Star's champion bloodlines and success on the track—but still many thousands more than Sam could dream of obtaining in years, much less the next few weeks. She let out her breath in a slow sigh. "Thanks for the info."

"No problem." Kate sent Sam a sympathetic smile. "I could talk to my dad for you. Maybe he could shave a bit off the price for you and your mom."

"Unless he shaved off half, it wouldn't really matter." Sam forced a laugh. "But thanks for the thought."

"Call me tomorrow." Kate started walking backward to the parking lot. "And watch out for greenhorns!" She grinned before slipping inside the cab of her pickup.

Sam waved, then grimaced as the door to Suite A opened and Ethan stepped onto the porch. She probably should apologize to him. Her mouth was always getting her in trouble, and her mom had a point—the Ames family had the potential to be big tippers. The last thing the farm needed was their sudden departure—especially over something Sam said.

She sighed and trudged toward the cabin. Time to cowboy up.

Ethan let the cabin door slam behind him as he stepped outside onto the porch. The term *suite* had to be a joke—or else the Jensons had never been in a real city before. A suite meant space. Not semi-new bathtubs and adjoining porches. He'd also have to share the bathroom with Daniel. At least he was far enough away from the adjoining cabin not to hear his parents fight. Unless they were making money, they were fighting—and with Jeffrey remaining unconvinced this venture would turn a profit, the arguments were already starting. They had to secure this property as quickly and as cheaply as they could in order to ensure a profit large enough to make it worthwhile in Jeffrey's eyes. But his mother would win. She always did.

Ethan gripped the wooden railing, staring out across the green meadow. Horses grazed, their tails swishing at flies, while a fiery July sun set behind the farthest hill. The longer Ethan watched, the looser his grip became, until finally his shoulders relaxed and he breathed deeply. Maybe there was something to this country air thing after all. Ethan would never admit it in front of Daniel—or his parents—but sometimes, he wished for something other than the late nights in his office, pushing paperwork to further pad his father's bank account. There had to be more to life than money. The church he'd once attended as a child with his grandmother confirmed that suspicion, but once Ethan hit the work world after graduating, time for God seemed to be crowded out as deadlines and marketing the business took first priority.

A paint horse whinnied from the pen, and Ethan studied the brown-and-white animal through narrowed eyes. If Ethan stretched low, really low to the depths of all his childhood memories, he'd admit to having cowboy dreams once upon a time. What little boy didn't? He used to squirrel away books on horses, Jessie James and the Old West, tucking them inside textbook covers so his father would think he was reading "productively." When Ethan reached high school, girls and cars became top priority until his gun-slingin', lassoing, bareback riding dreams were all but forgotten.

Until he pulled up on the ranch and breathed the air laden with horse sweat, leather and dust. Now those dreams were slowly resurrecting, a fact that would have Daniel doubled over with laughter and his dad smirking beneath that thick mustache. What would it be like to have the freedom to chase his dreams, rather than follow his father's plans? Ethan didn't want to take over Ames Real Estate and Development.

He didn't know yet that he wanted to ride a horse for a living, either, but surely there was something in between.

Footsteps thudded on the porch stairs and Ethan turned with a start. Samantha—no, Sam—joined him on the porch, her hands shoved in the back pockets of her jeans.

"Back for more insults?" Ethan shifted to face her, resting his weight against the railing and crossing his arms over his chest. His heart thudded louder than her boots on the wood floor—real working boots, not the useless designer ones Daniel brought.

Ethan fought to keep his expression neutral, his mind reliving Sam's snappy comment from earlier in the day. No woman had ever spoken to him with such an attitude before, and to be honest, he was impressed. Sam was different from other women he knew—that was certain—and it had nothing to do with her cowboy hat or plaid Western button-down.

Sam's chin lifted a fraction as she stopped a few feet away. "I came to apologize. You're our guest, and I was rude." Her lips twitched. "I just really don't like being called Samantha."

"I gathered that." Ethan tapped his chin, pretending to be in deep thought. "Why not a compromise—Sammy?"

Sam rolled her eyes. "Just stick with Sam and we won't have any problems, okay?"

"Deal." Ethan studied her guarded pose, then held out his hand, for some reason anxious to make her smile. "Don't real cowboys shake on truces?"

Her brows rose. "I don't see a real cowboy here."

Ethan's hand fell to his side and Sam's eyes widened to giant blue orbs. "I'm so sorry, there I go again." She slapped her hand over her mouth and groaned. "I don't mean to—I just—"

"Have a lot of pent-up frustration?"

Her arm lowered. "You have no idea."

"Don't worry about it." Ethan shoved aside the bruised portion of his pride and shot Sam a sideways glance. "Samantha."

Her eyes, greenish now that anger sparked inside, narrowed. "You're impossible." She clomped back down the porch steps and Ethan watched her leave, an unexplainable joy rising in his chest at having gotten to her once again.

"See you on the trail, partner." Ethan grinned as he braced his arms on the porch railing and watched her stalk to the main house. He had a feeling this working vacation was just getting started in more ways than one.

Chapter Three

Sam was up at dawn the next morning, partially because of her growling stomach and the full schedule for the day and partially because Ethan's face had teased her dreams all night. There was nothing worse than tossing and turning in the midst of a dream you didn't want to have—make that a nightmare. Who did Ethan Ames think he was, riding into her life as if he belonged there? So what if he was handsome? There wasn't enough room in all of Texas for the size of his ego. Teasing her about her name, as if he should automatically be granted special privileges, was the last straw in Sam's hay bale of tolerance. If money meant instant ego, Sam was glad she hovered on the poor side of the spectrum.

But poor wasn't going to bring back her father's legacy.

Sam dressed quickly in jeans and a button-down, then grabbed her cowboy hat off her dresser. Her eye caught the photo of her dad, taken nearly twenty years ago at the height of his rodeo fame, and she gently touched the worn wooden frame. She often wondered what their lives would be like if her father hadn't quit the circuit when she turned seven. Would she and her mom still be following him around in that beat-up RV, touring city after city, winning prize after prize? Maybe if her dad hadn't quit and taken over his grandfather's breeding farm to provide a safe life for his family, he'd still be alive.

The irony was what ate at Sam for years, and still occasionally nibbled on her thoughts. Wade Jenson gave up his dreams and his talent to avoid danger and be there for his family—yet the tragic accident happened during his first tribute appearance years after quitting. Angie had told him not to ride, that he hadn't in too long and it'd be dangerous. But Wade Jenson was never one to displease a begging crowd of fans, so he took on the infamous bull Black Thunder. It was the last time he ever rode anything. The injuries from being trampled lingered, and Sam and Angie spent the next several weeks at the hospital until Wade's body gave out—along with their family savings.

What if Wade had recovered, and the breeding farm could have continued as planned? What if Sam didn't have to help her mother carry the burden of providing for their livelihood, and could have moved out? Gone to college? Felt free to date and marry?

She turned away from the picture before the familiar sting of tears could burn her eyes, and shoved her cowboy hat on her head. She was through with the what-ifs. All that mattered were the what-nows. And right now, she had a trail ride to lead, an annoying man to ignore and a farm to save.

Sam pressed her knee into Piper's side, waiting for him to exhale before tightening the girth of the saddle. The paint gelding was known for holding his breath during the tacking process, leaving a loose, comfortable girth and a rider hanging on for dear life. "I know your game, boy. Give it up."

Piper exhaled in defeat and Sam quickly cinched the girth strap. She rubbed briskly under Piper's mane, her fingers immediately coated with sweat and little white and brown hairs. "Just a short trip, boy. I know it's hot out here." Even though it was only nine-thirty on a Friday morning, the summer sun inched along its path in the sky, blazing the ranch with heat. Only a handful of tourists had shown up for the ride—unfortunately, Vickie and Ethan Ames included.

Sam gathered the reins and clicked her tongue at Piper. He followed her to the edge of the paddock, where she looped the reins around the hitching post. After last night's drama with Ethan on the porch and her round of bad dreams, she'd hoped he'd sleep in and mercifully spare her his presence at the morning ride. He'd skipped breakfast, so Sam figured there was a good chance. But no, there he stood beside Vickie, dressed in designer jeans and a short-sleeved polo shirt that revealed the tanned lines of muscle in his arms.

Sam adjusted the blanket under Piper's saddle with a sharp tug. Where did a city boy like Ethan get a tan? Must be all that driving with the convertible top down. She would imagine he hadn't earned it with sweat and honest work.

Same with the muscles.

"Is that my horse for today?" Vickie Ames gestured to Piper.

Sam nodded and introduced the painted gelding to Vickie. "He's a sweetie, sort of like a big puppy. Just don't spook him with any sudden noises." All the working ranch horses were docile and well-trained, but they still had spunk. Piper hated loud noises, a fact he reminded them of every time it thundered. Sam had fixed more than her share of stall doors and fences after one of Piper's episodes.

"Of course I won't." Vickie patted Piper's nose, then winced at her hair-covered hand. "I forgot my handkerchief."

"Use your jeans, Mom." Ethan sidled up to the paddock fence beside Sam. He winked. "Good morning, Sam."

Sam gritted her teeth, remembering how her mother had specifically asked her to be nice. Her mother was right across the corral, so Sam better fake it for a while. She drew a deep breath. "Mornin'."

"Where's my horse?"

Sam pointed to a chestnut mare that Cole Jackson, one of the longtime stable hands, was saddling a few feet away. "You'll be riding Miss Priss."

"Miss Priss?" Ethan smiled. "You did that on purpose, didn't you?"

Sam shrugged, not wanting to admit he was right. The mare's name was girlie, but the older horse was stubborn. Sam had a feeling if anyone could put Ethan in his place, it would be Miss Priss.

"Well, I'm sure me and the little lady will get along great." Ethan brushed his hands on his jeans with a pointed look at his mom, who was still picking horse hair off her palm.

"Mrs. Ames, would you like help mounting?" Sam turned her back to Ethan.

Vickie looked up with a relieved smile. "That would be great. I don't know if you can tell, but I'm not used to being around horses much."

No kidding. Sam worked to keep her smile natural as she boosted the woman into the saddle, glad Vickie was at least wearing jeans and riding boots, even if they did look so new she'd surely have a blister by the end of the ride. Angie made a point of stating on the ranch's Web site to bring comfortable, worn-in clothing for riding, but ninety percent of their guests ignored the suggestion and were usually miserable by the end of the week. Sam had never understood the fashion-over-function mindset.

Beside her, Cole shook back his dark hair in frustration as if he'd noticed the same thing. "Greenhorns," he mumbled as he handed the reins to another tourist.

"Can I get a leg up, too?"

Sam ignored Ethan's taunting call from two horses away, focusing on adjusting the stirrup length for Vickie instead. He was apparently determined to get to her again today, and Sam was just as determined not to let him.

"You know, since I'm not a *real* cowboy." His teasing continued.

Sam moved to work on the second stirrup, keeping her eyes averted from Ethan's position beside Miss Priss. *Ignore him, ignore him.* Cole could help him mount. Not that Ethan actually needed help mounting, he just wanted to rub in Sam's face her verbal mistake from last night.

"Please, *Samantha?*"

Sam dropped the stirrup abruptly, jostling Vickie's leg, and glared across the fence at Ethan. "You know, I thought they said mules were stubborn. Not—"

Angie bumped into Sam as she appeared next to her, effectively cutting off Sam's sentence. "Lovely day, isn't it, Mrs. Ames? Hot, but beautiful. That's Texas for you." Angie finished adjusting the stirrup and shot Sam a warning look. "Go help him," she whispered. She smiled back up at Mrs. Ames. "I love that blouse."

Sam rubbed her face with both hands before slowly walking to Ethan's side, leaving her mother and Vickie chatting about clothing labels in her wake. She hated that her mother had arrived to hear her comment. *God, I'm losing it. Please cool my temper. I don't know why this guy gets to me so badly.* Sam sucked in a fresh breath of air and forced a smile at Ethan. "Need a leg up, you said?"

"Nah, I got it now." He swung into the saddle and reached down to adjust his heel in the stirrup.

Sam fought to keep the shock off her face and nodded stiffly. "Fine." She *knew* he'd been faking asking for assistance. Sam felt Ethan's eyes on her back as she quickly moved to finish saddling Diego, and stifled a groan. This was going to be the world's longest trail ride.

Would this trail ride never end? Ethan shifted in the saddle and his thigh muscles screamed in discomfort. How did Sam do it? She rode like she'd been born in a saddle, leading their small group through the shaded woods, pausing occasionally to gesture to a particular grouping of trees or a historical marker. Her back stayed straight, her hips relaxed, moving like she and that red horse were one being.

He and Miss Priss, however, were getting along more like a bull and a rodeo clown. He nudged her forward, she stopped. He pulled on the reins, she picked up her pace. He said "whoa," she tossed her head and insisted on moving forward.

Apparently real horses were nothing like that carousel his mother made him ride as a boy in Central Park—a fact Vickie must be realizing herself right about now. Ethan twisted around to catch a glimpse of his mom aboard Piper, one hand clutching the reins, the other in a white-knuckled grip on the saddle horn as the paint horse ambled along. At least Jeffrey had stayed at the cabin, determining that "appearances" could only be taken so far. No telling what Daniel had found to occupy his time. For all Ethan knew, the two could be plotting together a new scheme for making money. Jeffrey had always preferred Daniel's input on such concepts to Ethan's.

"We'll stop at the clearing ahead for a snack and to stretch our legs." Sam's voice rang from the front of the line, and Ethan could barely contain his relief.

As soon as the horses came to a stop in a flowered field, he slipped from the saddle, hoping Sam didn't notice the way his knees almost buckled when his shoes hit the grass. After the way he'd teased her earlier, he more than deserved any return insults.

There was also something intriguing about the fact that she hadn't shown any interest in Daniel. Usually women sensed him and his cousin's money a mile away. A cash radar, Daniel joked. He never seemed to mind, but Ethan wanted more. Was it possible he'd finally found someone oblivious to their financial charms?

Ethan pressed his hands into his lower back and stretched as the other riders were doing, then bent down and tried to touch his toes. Pain shot through his hamstrings, and he quickly straightened.

"Having trouble?" Sam appeared beside him, cheeks flushed with the summer heat, a water bottle dripping with condensation in one hand. She offered it to him.

He took the water with a tight smile and twisted off the cap. "Not at all." His right thigh suddenly cramped as if insisting otherwise. But he couldn't let Sam see his weakness, not after all the grief he'd given her. Apparently running on the treadmill required different muscles than horseback riding. He shifted uncomfortably.

"Good for you. So you'll have no trouble making it back? A lot of first time riders get pretty sore their first day on the trail." She took off her cowboy hat and shook her hair off her forehead. The feminine motion almost made Ethan forget her question.

He downed a quick sip of water to clear his head. "It'll be a piece of cake." More like a piece of prickly cactus.

Sam opened her mouth, probably to question his statement, but was interrupted by Vickie's yelp. Ethan turned to see his mother hanging half off Piper's saddle, one foot stretched toward the ground, the other stuck in the stirrup. Her dangling leg was at least a foot from the ground. "Help! He won't let me off!"

Her panicked cry flattened Piper's ears and the horse snorted in distress. Sam rushed to Vickie's side seconds ahead of Ethan, and grabbed Piper's reins. "Easy, boy." Her low tone perked Piper's ears, and he stopped the anxious shuffling of his legs.

Ethan helped support his mom's weight while Sam worked Vickie's boot free of the stirrup. Once her feet were on solid ground, she released a relieved sigh. "He started moving while I was getting down. I tried to get back on, but couldn't get enough momentum. He's so big!"

Sam's mouth twitched. Even Ethan could see Piper was several inches shorter than most of the other horses in the group. He patted his mother's arm. "You're safe now, don't worry."

"Do you want me to call the ranch to have someone pick you up?" Sam held Piper's reins, and the horse blew on her shoulder. She didn't even flinch as his flabby lips worked against her hair. How did she know those giant horse teeth wouldn't sink into her neck?

Vickie brushed the front of her stiff jeans. "I'll be fine. Walking around a little will help."

"It's good to keep moving," Sam agreed. "There are water bottles and packages of crackers in my saddle bag. Please help yourself."

Vickie thanked her and headed in that direction, while Sam briefly closed her eyes and exhaled.

Ethan quirked an eyebrow. "Something wrong?"

"I warned her not to make any sudden or loud noises." Sam patted Piper's hairy cheek. "He's skittish about that. She really could have gotten hurt."

Ethan remembered all the times growing up where his mother's voice had startled him, as well, and he reached out to rub Piper's ear. "Hey, I can relate." He smiled at Sam.

The edges of her mouth started to curl in response, but just as suddenly, she gathered Piper's reins. "Let's get you grazing with the other horses." She clucked twice to the paint before leading him away—without a second glance at Ethan.

Sam's heart raced, and it wasn't from the near incident with Mrs. Ames and Piper. No, it had everything to do with that brown-eyed stranger and his deadly smile. She pressed a hand against her stomach and drew a tight breath. So what if Ethan was handsome? She'd been around attractive men before, and most of them turned out to be completely full of themselves. If she had time for romance—which she didn't—she needed a man who spent more time outdoors than looking in a mirror. Attractive or not, Ethan Ames was still a rich guy bent on teasing her. He might have had a humane moment there, relating to Piper, but she couldn't forget the incessant teasing he'd doled out to her earlier that morning while saddling up.

Sam tugged on Piper's reins, urging the paint to follow. There was the point, however, that Ethan could have gotten angry with Sam for venting about his mother, and didn't. That showed something decent lurked in the heart underneath that polo shirt of his. Regardless, she'd have to watch her mouth around the tourists from now on. Her unedited remarks could easily come back to bite her—and the ranch's business.

Piper snorted as Sam released him next to the other horses in the field. His black patches gleamed in the noon sun, reminding Sam of Noble Star's midnight-blue coat. She'd better quit wasting time thinking about Ethan and focus on finding a way to earn money to purchase the stallion. She needed a plan, and fast—before someone else realized the stallion's worth and beat Sam to it. He could very well be the ticket for getting them out of their financial crisis.

The wind lifted Sam's hair and cooled her neck. She soaked in the breeze, tilting her face to the sun, and then turned back to the group of riders just in time to see Ethan look quickly away from her.

Sam started back toward the tourists, purposefully heading away from Ethan. If she wasn't careful, *he* could very well be the ticket for messing up her plans—and her heart.

Chapter Four

The alarm clock on the nightstand glowed three o'clock in bright green digital numbers. Sam sat up in bed, wide-awake. She should have been out the moment her weary shoulders hit the mattress, but her mind kept racing with the events of the day. The trail ride. Ethan. Mrs. Ames scaring the horses. Chores, both inside the house and out. Ethan. Answering the tourists' endless questions about ranch life. Helping Cole finish mucking out stalls. Ethan.

His creeping into her thoughts was even more annoying than the fact that she couldn't sleep.

Sam clicked on the lamp, and then slowly slid to the floor. Sitting cross legged, she reached under the bed. The navy dust ruffle was, ironically, covered in dust, and she sneezed. Who had time to vacuum under the beds when there was so much else to do? Wishing for a housekeeper was ridiculous when they were having trouble even paying their mortgage, but Sam couldn't help but wish anyway. Her searching fingers found the edge of the cardboard box and she tugged it free.

Shiny gold medals stared back at her as she peered over

the rim. This was foolish, going through her father's box of rodeo awards in the middle of the night. She hadn't pulled the box out in months, not since Angie finally took them down from their display in the den. Her mother had put the box in the storage shed, but Sam had snuck back outside and grabbed it hours later. She could understand her mother needing to pack it away, needing closure, but the contents of the box represented her dad. Painful as it was to sift through the mementos, Sam at least wanted the option of doing so.

She ran her fingers over an engraved belt buckle. BULL RIDING CHAMPION, 1990. Another medal. SECOND PLACE TEAM ROPING, 1985. Several ribbons nestled inside the box, along with her dad's bull-riding gloves and his favorite black cowboy hat. A local newspaper article about his tragic death lay on the very bottom, and Sam quickly covered it up with the hat. It was too late at night for that level of emotion.

She picked up the flyer advertising the annual Appleback Rodeo, dated over two years ago, and smiled. Bittersweet memories. Every year, the town of Appleback hosted a two-week series of events, starting with the Appleback Street fair, ending with the infamous rodeo, and offering a string of cooking and eating contests, concerts and everything else one could imagine in between.

Sam absently traced the lariat border design on the flyer. Once upon a time, she had dreamed dreams similar to her father's. As a child she loved riding, roping and all things adventurous. One of her favorite childhood pictures was her and her dad on horseback, Sam wearing nothing but a diaper and a big baby grin. Wade Jenson taught Sam to ride not many years later, and she barrel-raced in local junior rodeos until she turned sixteen. Even after her dad quit the rodeo circuit, his tips and tricks still seemed to subconsciously leak out of his sentences. *Heels down, Sam. Don't look at your rope, look at your target. You'll never earn the title of Rodeo Sweetheart with that form. Let go of that saddle horn, girl, what are you afraid of?* Sam eventually felt more comfortable around horses than people—a fact she proved by skipping her prom to tend to a new baby foal, and standing up more than one date in favor of helping her dad trailer horses to a new client.

When Wade passed away, the thrill seeker in Sam died along with him. She watched herself—and her life—slow down until it nearly stopped. Afternoons galloping bareback across meadows were suddenly spent soaping up saddles and hosing down horses. The chores had to get done, but she could have snuck away for some fun once in a while. Could have—but didn't. Fun meant danger, and that first year after Wade's death, Sam couldn't even mount a horse without thinking of her dad. It seemed wrong to be the same person she always was when he wasn't there to see it, wasn't there to offer his advice and big congratulatory hugs.

Sudden tears stung her eyes and Sam's grip tightened on the advertisement in her hands. The annual rodeo was coming up in August—only a few weeks away. A couple of years ago, she would have entered the barrel racing or roping competition as usual, and would have already been practicing for months.

The writing on the flyer blurred before her eyes, and Sam blinked rapidly to clear the moisture clouding her vision. Her life wasn't about the rodeo anymore, couldn't ever be again. Even if she wanted to compete, Angie would never allow it. At twenty-four, Sam was obviously long past grounded as a means of discipline, but putting disappointment or fear in her mother's eyes was far worse than any childhood punishment. Things changed, and Sam had to change right along with them.

She started to put the flyer back in the box, but the bold

numbers on the bottom stopped her hand midreach and Sam's eyes widened. Things changed, all right. The grand prize a few years ago for the bull-riding competition was the exact amount she needed to buy Noble Star. Add two years' increase, and it was more than enough to get the breeding farm in the black.

The paper rustled as she stuffed the flyer in the box and shoved the entire thing under the bed. Maybe obtaining Noble Star wouldn't be a matter of luck after all, but rather, divine providence. Surely it wasn't coincidence about the money being the amount she needed. Was God finally going to offer assistance to get the Jenson family out of their financial crisis?

It'd be about time He stepped in.

Sam slipped beneath the cotton sheets and lay staring at the ceiling, arms crossed behind her pillow. Her heart hammered, and this time it wasn't from bad dreams, a busy day or thoughts of Ethan.

She had a plan.

The sun streamed through the miniblinds, scrawling patterns of light across the worn bedspread. Ethan grunted into his pillow but made no motion to move. He couldn't if he tried. He needed an ice pack. Or maybe a hot compress. Anything to ease the soreness that glazed his muscles with a constant, annoying ache.

He closed his eyes, then blinked them open at a snicker. Daniel sat on his bed a few feet away, pulling on his ridiculous boots and grinning. "You should have played darts at the lodge by the main house with me yesterday instead of going on that ride, man. I warned you."

Ethan pushed himself into a sitting position, wincing against the pain. He refused to look like a sissy in front of his cousin—but the grimace probably gave him away. "Yeah, right. You said be careful, riding a horse would make me sore. You didn't say riding a horse would make me feel like I'd been trampled by one."

Daniel shrugged as he stood. "I'm heading to the main house for breakfast. You coming, or do you prefer to limp around here instead?" His boots clomped on the wooden floor.

"I'll be there. Go ahead without me." Ethan slowly eased off the bed. "It'll take me a minute."

"Might be lunchtime before you make it."

"Very funny." Ethan winced. No wonder all the cowboys in those books he'd read as a child walked with such a wide stance. It was the only way to compensate. He swaggered toward the dresser and winced as he pulled out a pair of jeans.

Daniel tugged a cowboy hat down on his head and swiped his room key off the nightstand. "I'll save you some bacon."

"Why are you wearing all that stuff anyway?" Ethan gestured toward Daniel's Western gear, and his biceps quivered. Probably from that death grip he had on the saddle horn yesterday, despite making fun of his mom for doing the same. If Vickie felt even half as sore as he did, she'd probably already changed her mind about "appearances." He hated to agree with his dad on, well, anything—but this time, Jeffrey had a point about not all of them having to keep up the charade at every moment. Ethan would be more likely to see his dad hanging out the moon roof of a limo than he would ever see him aboard a horse.

Daniel tapped the brim of his hat. "Hey, I think I look good. Or at least, the girls I met at the lodge last night thought so." He winked.

"So that's why you stayed out so late." Mystery solved. Ethan shook his head and pulled on a green polo.

"Nothing wrong with mixing a little business with pleasure." Daniel paused at the front door. "Aren't you doing the same? I know you took that trail ride to check out the owner's daughter—Sarah, or whatever her name is."

Ethan worked to keep his expression neutral. "It's Sam—and hardly. I went riding so my mom wouldn't be alone."

Daniel's eyebrow twitched. "Right."

"Believe what you want. I have no interest in Sam." Her full name hovered on Ethan's lips and he couldn't but smile at her ire if he were to say it. Somehow, he suspected she could sense it even from across the ranch.

"Of course not. You always grin real goofy when you're not attracted to someone." Daniel rolled his eyes.

"Whatever." Ethan grabbed a pair of socks. It wasn't true—was it? Sure, Sam was pretty, and there was something different about her, something that went beyond the Western attire and massive chip on her shoulder. But Sam wasn't his type. So what if he'd wanted to tease her a little on the ride? There were worse motivations to have—and his had nothing to do with attraction. He was an Ames. An Ames wouldn't date a cowgirl.

Apparently, they just bought out their land.

Ethan brushed aside the sudden burst of conscience. It wasn't his plan, it was his dad's—not like Ethan had much of a choice. He never had, and at this rate, never would.

Daniel shook his head. "Send me a postcard from your vacation in denial, dude. I'm going to breakfast."

The front door had just shut behind him when a knock sounded. Ethan finished buckling his belt and opened the door. Jeffrey Ames waited with a frown on the other side. "Morning." Ethan fought back a sigh and moved aside for his father to enter.

Jeffrey strode inside the cabin with his usual air of dignified expectation. "What's wrong with you, boy?"

Ethan shut the door. "What do you mean?"

"You're moving like a robot."

"Sore muscles from the ride yesterday." Ethan eased onto the bed and reached for his loafers under the nightstand.

Jeffrey's frown deepened. "Your mother is fine."

"Mom does Pilates and yoga three times a week." Ethan slipped his feet inside the leather shoes, hoping his lowered head hid the shock he felt claiming his expression. His mom had always been a fitness guru, but he'd figured she'd be at least a little sore like he was. Was he that much of a Wild West sissy? He quickly stood, hoping to put an end to the conversation. "I was just heading to the main house to eat."

"I'll join you. But first, we need to talk." Jeffrey shoved his hands in his pockets of his slacks and jingled the loose change. The corners of his lips tightened beneath his mustache—the closest Ethan had ever seen his dad come to a real smile. "There's been a new development."

Ethan bit back a groan at the overused pun. "What's that?" Better not to encourage him with a forced laugh. Humor and Jeffrey Ames went together about as well as fast cars and speed limits.

Jeffrey's eyebrows furrowed. "I had a brief conversation with Angie Jenson yesterday. It seems like we're going to need more ammunition than we thought in order to convince that Jenson woman it's in her best interest to sell." His lips quirked. "To us."

"I don't get it. Why are you smiling? How is that good news?" Other than the fact they could possibly give up now and go back to New York. But for some reason, the thought of leaving so soon seemed more disappointing than alluring. Ethan frowned. Must be that country air getting to him. He needed Starbucks, a massage and a good couple miles on his treadmill. That'd get him back to thinking more like a businessman and less like John Wayne.

"It's good news because her daughter is the reason she's hesitating, and I now know who is going to help fix that." The twinkle was back in Jeffrey's eyes, and worry churned in Ethan's stomach.

"Who?" He didn't want to ask, but he and his father had played the cat-and-canary game for so long now, Ethan just automatically fluffed his feathers.

Jeffrey clamped his large hand on Ethan's shoulder, his diamond-and-gold ring digging into his collarbone. "You are."

Chapter Five

Sam still hadn't gotten used to eating her breakfast at a table full of strangers, but it beat sitting alone in her room. She scooped a spoonful of eggs on her plate and tried to ignore Daniel, who sat to her left, Ethan, who sat to her right, and Jeffrey, who chugged coffee directly across from her. Talk about a bad way to start her Sunday—sandwiched between two preppy, clueless tourists. Daniel had been trying to get her attention ever since he sat down, and Sam could have sworn she even saw him flexing beneath that striped Western shirt. Strangely enough, Ethan hadn't spoken a single word to her yet—just kept darting glances at his dad across the table. Jeffrey in turn would cough and send pointed glares right back.

Men could be so weird.

Sam peppered her eggs and focused her attention on the other end of the large table. Her mom nibbled delicately at a piece of bacon while the same flirtatious man from yesterday—Mike—chatted her up. His troublemaking, ball-kicking son, Davy, sat ignored to his left, building a waffle sculpture on a plate covered in syrup. The sculpture wobbled on its liquid foundation, and if Sam's predictions were accurate, it would go sloshing into Mike's lap any minute now. It would serve him right.

She blew out her breath in an impatient huff. At least the group of vacationing, giggly college-aged girls were absent from breakfast this morning—the ones she'd seen Daniel eye more than once. It also appeared that their resident honeymoon couple was sleeping in. Sam really missed the mornings when Sunday breakfast consisted of just her and her parents—not a host of strangers and hired help. Sure, the food was better now than the cold cereal or lumpy oatmeal they used to have before rushing off to church, but it had been family. Familiar. It had been home.

A concept that apparently died along with her dad.

Sam gave a tired smile to Clara, the newly hired cook, who hovered over Sam's shoulder with a fresh pot of coffee.

"Refill?"

"Yes, thanks." Sam inched her cup closer. She needed the caffeine after last night's 3:00 a.m. stroll down memory lane. If her family went to church anymore, she'd probably have yawned through the entire service. But the work—and the animals—couldn't wait, and with the addition of a busy new dude ranch came the loss of a church home for Sam, at least until they could afford to hire more help. But despite the fact she couldn't quit yawning, the emotional journey last night had been worth it. She knew how to get the money to buy Noble Star. She just needed a fresh supply of courage—and someone to help her.

Clara stretched over with the coffeepot. "Not a problem, Ms. Sam." The hot liquid bubbled into the mug.

"You can just call me Sam." She lowered her head and breathed in the hearty aroma of the brew. One sip of that strong concoction and she'd wake up for sure.

"Okay." Clara moved to refill Daniel's cup. Her tight black curls and ebony skin heightened her youthful appearance, but Sam knew Clara had to be closer to a grandma's age herself. She nodded at Daniel. "Coffee?"

Daniel shook his head, his mouth full of toast. "I've reached my limit." Crumbs sprayed on his nearly empty plate and Sam winced. And he wondered why his charms weren't working on her.

"I'll take a refill." Ethan twisted in his seat to offer his mug. His eyes caught Sam's and he smiled.

Sam decided to blame the accompanying jitters in her stomach on the greasy bacon, and forced a tight-lipped smile in return before focusing once again on her food. The eggs were suddenly tasteless in her mouth despite the salt and pepper she'd heaped on them. She was probably too nervous too eat. She really needed to talk to Cole about her plan before the day got fully started. If he refused to help her, she'd be right back to square one.

The fact that Ethan's presence radiated on Sam's right side like a portable heater had nothing to do with her lack of appetite. Nothing at all.

"Samantha?" Ethan's quiet voice sounded in her ear.

She dropped her fork with a clatter. "It's Sam. Why is that so hard for you? I don't call you Evan, or Eric. My name is Sam. You want me to start calling you Elvira?"

Ethan held up both hands in defense, eyes wide. "I'm sorry. It was an accident."

"I bet." Sam tossed her napkin on her plate. She needed to find Cole, now—before she lost her opportunity to talk to him alone and before she completely snapped and threw a piece of bacon in Ethan's face. Never in her life had anyone so adamantly insisted on calling her Samantha. That was her father's right, and no loafer-wearin' city boy was going to take that away.

"It really was a slipup. Look, I was going to ask if you wanted to take a walk. Show me around the ranch or whatever."

Sam studied Ethan. His cheeks pinked the longer she stared, and the expression in his eyes didn't quite match his tone. He looked guarded—almost annoyed. She glanced across the table at Jeffrey, who beamed and nodded at his son.

Something was up. Sam shoved her chair away from the table. "Sorry, I've got things to do."

"Sam!" Angie looked up from the other end of the table in surprise. "Don't be rude." Mike smirked and Sam wished she could shove her mother's glittering diamond ring in his face.

"Duty calls, Mom." Sam gulped a mouthful of coffee, then wished she'd let it cool just a moment longer. Refusing to water down her dramatic exit with a wince, she stoned her features, bumped her chair under the table with a scrape and stalked toward the back door.

The satisfying slosh of waffles and syrup, followed by Mike's squeal, sounded just before the door slammed shut behind her.

Rejected. Ethan excused himself from the breakfast table and hustled—well, limped was probably more accurate—outside before his dad could finish his breakfast and come after him. Ethan refused to stick around for a lecture on failure from his father. Before breakfast, his dad had directed Ethan to strike up a friendship with Sam in order to make Sam's mom see her having a good time. One of the reasons Angie was considering selling the ranch over Sam's objections was because she wanted her daughter to have a chance to live her life and not be burdened by a failing business. It was also his chance to get inside information about the ranch. Any pitfalls, any problems, any information that could be useful for their securing a low offer on the property was now Ethan's job to report.

Ahead of him, Sam blazed a trail to the barn as if her boots were on fire. It was surprising the grass at her feet didn't puff up in smoke as she passed. Ethan hesitated. He'd never been the type to pursue a woman scorned—Shakespeare definitely had that one right—and that's exactly what he'd done to Sam with his incessant teasing.

But Shakespeare hadn't met Jeffrey Ames, and any minute now, his father would be about five steps behind Ethan, demanding to know why he wasn't trying harder to weasel into a friendship with Sam.

Ethan kicked at a rock in the dirt with his loafer. Take a walk? Pretty lame. Not really surprising Sam turned him down after that ridiculous attempt. He really hadn't meant to say her full name, it just slipped out while he was mentally rehearsing his next line.

A rehearsal that led to a less than successful opening curtain. Why was she so picky about her name, anyway? Samantha was a beautiful name. He understood she was a tomboy, a cowgirl, but that shouldn't be enough to make her hate her full name. It didn't make sense.

Sort of like how what happened at breakfast wouldn't make sense to his dad. Ethan could just hear his response now. *Daniel wouldn't have that kind of problem with a woman. Daniel could get any girl he wanted. You should learn from your cousin.* Yeah, right. One day Daniel and Jeffrey both would wake up and realize there were more important things in the world than money and manipulative games. One day they'd come to the same conclusion Ethan eventually had come to—that they wanted something more from life than just a trust fund, a successful if borderline shady business and empty relationships.

If you could even call them relationships. Ethan lifted his face to the morning sun and let the warm summer breeze dry the sweat on his forehead. He wasn't foolish enough to believe his parents lived in marital bliss. He purposefully tuned out the details he didn't want to know.

His parents were glued together only by money, and if that ever changed, they'd probably head to divorce court faster than a Ferrari off the line. Ethan wanted something more solid than that, something to really stand on. No wonder he'd never felt a true connection before with the girls in his past—as much as he loved his mother, they all seemed like carbon copies of her. Materialistic, superficial.

Every girl but Sam, that is.

He shoved his hands in his pockets and continued his slow trek to the barn. He could move out and avoid the drama, but his parents' house was big enough for him to be out of the way, and it was rent-free. If he hoped to break away from the family business one day, he'd more than likely be cut off financially and would need a decent amount of cash saved—in a place his father couldn't access. All the more reason to save money now.

A horse whinnied from the other side of a nearby fence, and Ethan squared his shoulders in determination. His plan A in reaching Sam might have been a bust, but that didn't mean plan B couldn't succeed. If he needed to amp up the flirty image, so be it. Ethan hated the pretense—it reeked of Daniel—but if it would get his father off his back, then it'd be worth it. Plus he'd like to see her smile more. No twenty-four-year-old should have to work so hard just to stay afloat.

He just needed to remember not to use her full name.

Ethan turned up the collar on his polo, cracked his neck and strode inside the barn with a slightly crooked smile.

"Crazy city slickers." Sam ran the grooming brush over Wildfire's back in short, firm strokes. Loose hair flurried in her face like miniature red snowflakes, but she didn't care. Who did Ethan think he was, asking her to go for a walk while his father grinned from the sidelines? The invitation was probably a joke, some "let's tease the cowgirl and make her think I'm interested" ploy so he and his dad could laugh behind her back later. Like she'd ever be interested in some New Yorker who didn't know which end of the horse went first.

Sam brushed faster. The only bright spot on this cloudy morning was that Cole had agreed to help her out. The loyal stable hand had assured her he'd have a steer in the north paddock by eleven o'clock that night for her to practice riding, and that her secret was safe with him. Apparently Cole hated dealing with the downfalls of the new dude ranch business as much as Sam and was game for her plan—absurd as it must have sounded.

She looked up as a dark figure, silhouetted by the sun, strolled inside the barn. The cocky gait seemed familiar, and within moments Ethan's features became distinguishable. *Great.* He was back for round two. She kept brushing and refused to acknowledge his presence.

Ethan stopped in front of Wildfire's stall and hooked his arms over the closed gate. "Mornin', again." He smiled and Sam couldn't help her eyes darting to meet his. She quickly ducked under Wildfire's neck to groom his other side. It put her closer to Ethan but at least her back was to him.

"You missed one of the guests swimming in waffles."

Ethan's voice sounded smooth and rich over Sam's shoulder, much like the syrup that must be clinging to Mike's pants right about now. Too bad those waffles couldn't have fallen in Ethan's lap, too.

She dropped the grooming brush in the bucket in the corner behind her. "Sounds like fun." She bent and snatched a comb from the same tub, and began picking through Wildfire's tangled mane. "Is that all you came to tell me?" She felt more than saw Ethan's startled response, and couldn't but grin.

"No, I, just—well..." Ethan's voice trailed off and he coughed. "I thought maybe I could help out, if you were too busy to take a walk."

Sam turned to face him, the blue comb dangling from her fingers. Even Wildfire snorted, as if shocked. "You want to do chores?"

"Sure." Ethan straightened his slumped position on the gate and smiled. "Why not?"

"Why not?" Sam laughed as she turned back to Wildfire's mane. "Because you have no clue what you're doing. Because you could get hurt. Because this is your vacation and you shouldn't be working. Because—"

"Okay, I get it." Ethan held up both hands. "But I don't mind. I can learn."

"Thanks, but no thanks." Sam tossed the comb in the bucket and clipped the lead rope that she'd draped over the stall door to Wildfire's halter. "Excuse me."

Ethan backed away from the gate as Sam and Wildfire walked through, giving Wildfire's back legs a wide berth. "Then what about a walk later tonight? After dinner?" His tone held a hopeful edge.

Sam clucked to Wildfire and led him down the barn aisle. His shoed hooves clacked on the hard floor. "Again, thanks—

but no thanks." Sam refused to feel even slightly sympathetic or look back at Ethan standing alone in the barn aisle. She had zero interest in being a pawn for some rich boy's family to manipulate with their weird games. She had chores to do, a ranch to save and a bull to ride.

Starting with a steer tonight at eleven o'clock.

Chapter Six

The moon hung low in the velvet night sky, a shiny silver orb against a sea of black. Sam trudged through the shadows toward the north paddock, her boots silent on the dewy grass. Despite the late hour, adrenaline pulsed in her veins and her hands shook. She shoved them into the back pockets of her jeans as she walked.

Maybe she was crazy. Riding a steer was nothing like riding a bull, as steers were significantly smaller, but it was all she had access to for practice. She'd sat on a bull once before on a dare—for about two seconds at a friend's ranch as a young teenager. Of course, that was before her friend's father ran outside, yelling at them for taking the risk and looking much scarier than the bull. After watching the competition at the local rodeo each year, Sam figured her brief stint couldn't even come close to being the same.

She rounded the corner of the barn, and the outline of the steer's narrow horns inside the paddock siphoned into view. Cole, dressed in dark denim from head to foot, waited by the fence, one boot hung lazily on the bottom rail. A long rope was coiled over his shoulder. He straightened as she approached. “You ready for this, kid?”

Sam nodded. Only Cole could get away with such a nickname. He’d started work at the Jenson farm right after he graduated high school, when Sam was a child, and stayed on full-time these past twenty years. Now he was more like a big brother than a hired hand. “Of course I’m ready. Bring it.”

The tremor in Sam’s voice almost cancelled out the confident words, but to her relief, Cole didn’t seem to notice. “That’s what I like to hear.” He opened the paddock gate and motioned for Sam to go through first.

She strode into the pen, keeping a wary eye on the steer. The miniature beast looked up from inside the makeshift chute Cole had concocted, and blinked lazily, grass dangling from its flabby lips. At this rate, riding would be a breeze—downright boring, even. But once Cole tied that rope around the steer’s hindquarters…Sam swallowed. “Where’d you get him?”

“A friend with a cattle ranch a few miles west owed me a favor. He said we can borrow Lucy here for as long as we’d like.”

“Lucy?”

“Short for Lucifer.” Cole winked.

Sam’s stomach flipped.

“I know he looks calm now, but this here is a flank strap.” Cole gestured with the fleece-lined leather rope he uncoiled off his shoulder. “Don’t worry. It’ll get him bucking good.”

That was the problem. Sam forced a smile, hoping the evening shadows hid her apprehension. She couldn’t back down now, not after Cole had gone to all that effort to bring the beast. Besides, kids rode steers in rodeos all the time—it was considered a junior event. If some 4-H preteen could do it, Sam could, too.

She just wouldn’t think about her father’s last bull ride in the process.

"What do we do first?" Sam crossed her arms, hoping to keep her pounding heart from bursting through her long-sleeved T-shirt. Too bad Cole couldn't have found a steer with shorter horns.

Cole started toward the animal, which backed up a step. "I'll tie the flank strap and bull rope on him, and you hop on."

"And then what?"

"Hang tight." Cole grinned, his teeth a white splash against dark stubble.

Easy for him to say. He wasn't about to mount a giant cow with horns. Sam took a deep breath as Cole straddled the fencing between the rail and the makeshift pen and went to work securing the flank strap. Cowboy up, as her father always said. She could do it—for him, for the farm. Winning the rodeo competition was her only immediate chance at earning enough money to buy Noble Star from Kate's dad. Without the stallion, the farm would continue having to front as a tourist trap. Going from trail rider to bull rider would be hard enough with months of training—and Sam only had a few weeks. There was no time to waste.

"All set." Cole gave a final tug on the rope and sat back on the fence. The steer snorted his disapproval. "Need a leg up?"

She ran her hands down the front of her jeans. *Get on the steer, Sam.* She took a steadying breath, trying to envision the finish line—Jenson Farms, back the way it used to be. "Sure." She climbed the fence before she could change her mind, and hooked one leg over the top rail. Holding on to Cole's arm for balance, she brought in her outside leg and eased onto the steer's leathery back. Heavy muscles twitched under her weight.

Sam gripped the bull rope around the steer's neck and held tight, just as Cole advised. "Any last words of wisdom?" Her voice shook again and this time she didn't care.

Cole shrugged. "Don't fall off?"

"Thanks." Her nervous laugh punctured the weighty silence resting on her shoulders and she rotated her neck. She could do this. It was a new adventure, one she probably would have pursued long before now if things had turned out differently for her family. No reason to be scared—as long as those horns stayed up there with the steer's head where they belonged.

"Ready?" Cole hopped from the fence to the dirt, patchy with mud from a recent rain, and reached over to unlatch the chute's gate.

Yes. No. Never. She squeezed her eyes shut and nodded.

Her world exploded.

Hooves thundered. Dirt pelted her face. Sam's arm wrenched against the bull rope, yet her fingers refused to let go. She clung tighter with her legs and forced her eyes open. Sky, earth. Sky, earth. It was like riding a hairy, out-of-control rocking chair. How could her dad have ever done this for fun?

The steer snorted, his horns twisting to the left and then to the right. Sam bounced hard against his thick neck. From her peripheral vision, she glimpsed Cole clapping his hands. "You're doing great!"

She was? Maybe she could do this after all. Her biceps screamed in protest and Sam winced as mud slung in her face. She instinctively twisted away from the dirty onslaught just as Lucy turned—in the opposite direction.

Sam hit the ground hard, mud oozing into her ears and down the neck of her shirt. She raised her hands to protect her face, but Lucy, free of her burden, had harmlessly trotted back toward the chute.

Sam lowered her hands, aware of a fiery ache in her quivering right arm and thighs, aware of Cole yelling for her not to get up yet, aware that had she been thrown just a few feet farther to the left, she would have landed on the paddock rails.

But mostly, she was aware of Ethan Ames standing on the other side of the fence, his face a mixture of shock and amusement.

Ethan wasn't sure if he should offer his hand, laugh or run away. He was tempted to do all three. But the stable hand he recognized from the trail ride yesterday beat him to his first instinct, and pulled Sam out of the dirt.

"What are you doing here?" Her wary eyes met Ethan's as she slapped at the mud clinging to her jeans.

Ethan braced both arms against the top rail dividing them. "The better question is why are you riding a bull?" Dirt speckled Sam's honey-colored hair, but he wasn't about to point that out.

"That ain't a bull, greenhorn." The stable hand spit in the paddock dirt. "That's a steer." He held Sam out in front of him by her shoulders. "Are you okay, kid? That was some fall."

"I'm fine, Cole." Sam wrestled out of his concerned grip, a dark red flush working up her neck. She met Ethan at the fence and glared. "Why are you up this late?"

Ethan checked the Rolex on his wrist, visible by the light of the moon. "Late? It's not even midnight."

Sam's eyes snapped. "Guests aren't supposed to be roaming the property all night long. This isn't a country club. People could get hurt."

"Hurt like when they fall off a bull?"

"It's a steer," Cole reminded.

"Bull, steer, cow, whatever." Ethan shrugged. "Why were you riding it?"

Sam hesitated.

"Trying to ride it, I guess I should say." If she wouldn't be honest, he couldn't help teasing her a little.

Sam's head jerked. "You want to give it a shot, if it's so easy?"

Ethan laughed. "No, thanks. I value my life."

"I do, too." Sam's voice quieted and she turned to stare toward the main house. "That's why I'm doing it."

Cole broke the ensuing silence. "Hey, kid, I'm gonna go put this steer up for the night."

"Wait, what if my mom—?" Sam's voice broke off and her eyes widened, flickering from Ethan, to the animal, to Cole.

Ethan frowned at the exchange. What was Sam worried about? More importantly, what was she so concerned about him knowing?

Cole strode toward the steer, which was now attempting to pull grass through the bottom rail of the paddock. His long horns knocked against the post and Ethan shuddered. What on earth could have possessed Sam to mount such an animal—practically in the middle of the night? There were obviously secrets here—maybe ones his father would be interested in. The faster this sale went through the faster he could break out on his own and leave Ames Real Estate and development in his dust.

"I'll handle it. Don't worry." Cole tipped his hat at Sam before reaching the animal. His low voice murmured softly through the night air, and the steer remained calm long enough for Cole to tug a rope around his neck and untie the one around his hind legs.

Something was definitely not right with this picture, and it had nothing to do with a steer-whispering stable hand. Ethan turned back to Sam. "Seriously, what's going on?"

"It's none of your business." She grabbed the fence and

began climbing over. Ethan sidestepped to avoid getting hit in the face with her swinging boot when she reached the top.

"Fine. I'll just go back to my cabin." Ethan walked backward two steps.

"Thank you." Sam landed on the ground and rubbed her right shoulder, which was more than likely bruised from her fall. She'd taken quite a hit. "See you tomorrow, I guess."

"No problem." Ethan turned, walking faster. He decided to take one last stab in the dark—literally. "I'm sure I can find out from Mrs. Jenson in the morning what all this was about."

Sam's hand snagged the back of his shirt and tugged, pulling Ethan to an abrupt halt. *Bingo.* He controlled his smile before turning around to meet her anxious expression.

"You can't ask her."

"Then tell me."

"I can't." Exasperation laced Sam's tone but Ethan stood his ground. If Sam confided in him, he'd be one step closer to friendship. One step closer to getting the information his dad needed before Jeffrey sent for backup—namely, Daniel.

The thought of Daniel weaseling his way into Sam's life sounded so much worse than Ethan doing the same. At least Ethan had no intentions of manipulating Sam's emotions. He just wanted to be friends, get the info his dad needed, and get back home to start his new life. Daniel, however, would prey on her emotions, attempt to mix business with pleasure and get something for himself from the deal. Ethan had to find out what Sam was up to first. His cousin had already taken enough from him, including Jeffrey's respect.

He didn't want Daniel anywhere near Sam.

He cleared his throat. "Why don't you want your mother to know?"

"I just don't. Are you going to tell her?"

"Maybe not, if you'll do something for me."

Sam crossed her arms. "What do you want out of this?"

What *did* he want? A gentle breeze caressed Ethan's neck and he shivered. He wanted to leave the real estate business, wanted to get as far away from his father as he could. He wanted to find what he was really good at and make an honest living, rather than be a pawn in his father's devious plans. He wanted independence, respect—and, watching the wind tease tendrils of hair around her dirt-streaked cheeks, what he really wanted was to kiss Sam.

He'd settle for two out of three. "I want to learn about ranching."

She snorted. "You can't be serious."

"I'm completely serious." Ethan straightened his shoulders, trying to imitate the way he'd seen Cole standing earlier—straight back, cocked hip, loose leg. Seeing the ranch from an insider's perspective would provide Ethan ample opportunity to discover any issues about the property his dad hoped to find. He'd do his job, make his father happy and get out of Dodge—or, rather Appleback—of his own will, and not because he was being replaced by Daniel. And maybe he could even show Sam how to enjoy life a bit and put a smile on her face. Everyone won.

Until your father buys Sam's beloved ranch.

Ethan quickly squelched the thought and held out his hand. "You teach me about horses and running a farm, and I'll keep your secret."

Sam shook on their deal. "You're rotten, you know that?"

Yes, Ethan did. Some days, he knew it all too well. That's why he needed to be free of his father's influence. He tightened his grip when Sam tried to pull her hand away. "One last condition."

Sam raised her eyebrows. Good thing looks couldn't actually kill. "What else could you possibly want?"

"I want you to tell me why you were riding that bull."

"Fine." She sighed.

"Promise?" He shook her hand again so she couldn't back out of the new condition. Weren't handshakes as good as a signed contract back in the Wild West days? He shook it harder.

"Promise." She wrestled her hand free and rubbed it.

"So why were you?" Ethan tilted his head, eager to hear what could possibly make a woman desperate enough to hop on a wild animal in the middle of the night with only the moon for a seatbelt.

"Why was I what?" Sam smirked and Ethan's smile slid off his face. "I promised to tell you why I was riding a bull. I never promised to tell you why I was riding a *steer*." She abruptly strode toward the barn.

Ethan ran his hands down the length of his face, once again not sure whether to laugh, go after her—or run far, far away.

Chapter Seven

A sudden pounding on the cabin door shook Ethan from a sound sleep. He groggily sat up in bed and moved to look out the front window. The sun was barely up—so why was he? The knocking continued.

"Coming!" He wiped at his bleary eyes. Daniel stirred under the covers from his bed across the room but didn't wake. Ethan threw on a pair of jeans and a T-shirt and yanked the door open with a scowl.

Sam stood on the front porch, hands tucked in the back pockets of her jeans, wearing a blue-and-white flowered button-down shirt that brought out her eyes. "Morning, sunshine."

Her smile, pretty as it might be, was much too bright this early on a Monday. "What do you want?"

"That's no way to greet your boss."

"Boss?" Ethan hit his ear with the palm of his hand, certain he'd heard wrong. His boss was his father, and Jeffrey Ames was thankfully nowhere in sight. What was Sam talking about?

"Well, maybe not boss, technically, because you're not

getting paid." Sam smirked. "But you are here to learn, so you're sort of like my apprentice—which means I'm in charge. Which means you need to get ready. We're behind schedule."

"Impossible. The sun just came up." Birds chirped from a nearby tree, and Ethan felt like throwing his pillow at them. He never fully woke up until consuming a massive amount of coffee—preferably Guatemalan dark roast, but he'd made do yesterday at the main house with the generic brand. Looked like he'd have to do it again.

Talk about living off the land.

"Ranchers get up before the sun, partner. Welcome to farm work." Sam quirked an eyebrow. "Of course, if you'd rather back out of our agreement..."

Agreements. Steers. Secrets. The previous night rushed at Ethan like a sports car on the autobahn and he groaned. No wonder he felt so exhausted. He'd gone back to bed after his midnight bargain with Sam, but had lain awake for at least another hour reliving his sudden rash of good luck. It was the perfect setup for getting his father off his back and putting his plan for future freedom into action. "You're not getting out of it. I'll be ready in two minutes." He closed the cabin door, leaving Sam to sulk on the porch. He refused to let her out of their deal—not when there was so much to lose.

Daniel sat up as Ethan flicked on the lamp and pulled a pair of socks from his dresser drawer. "What's going on, man? Breakfast isn't for another hour or more."

Ethan hesitated, hopping on one leg as he tugged his sock over his foot. He hated to tell Daniel the details of his arrangement, but Jeffrey would tell him eventually anyway. Besides, Daniel didn't have to know Ethan's true motivation for getting close to Sam—just the same reason that Jeffrey would hear. "I have a meeting with Sam." Hopefully that sounded vague enough to hide his growing feelings for her.

"Meeting, or date?" Daniel grinned, and then squinted outside. "Is the sun even up?"

"Meeting. Definitely just a meeting." Ethan slid into his loafers, thought better of it and grabbed his running shoes instead, the ones he'd ridden in two days ago. He hadn't packed cowboy boots—at the time, he hadn't imagined ever using them. Looked like he'd have to find a pair if he was going to be doing ranch work. At least these tennis shoes could get dirty with little consequence. He wrestled them on without untying the laces.

"What kind of meeting is worth a dawn appointment?" Daniel yawned and flopped back against his pillow. "You've got it bad, dude."

"You're dreaming—literally. Go back to sleep." Ethan automatically grabbed his watch, then realized there was no point in wearing it, not to do stable work. What exactly had he gotten himself into? This idea seemed much smarter in the middle of the night, staring at Sam's desperate blue eyes.

Sam didn't even bother to hide her smile as she watched Ethan grapple with the pitchfork inside Piper's stall. "You have to scoop it, Ethan. Not stab it." Across the pen, Piper flicked his tail as if agreeing.

"This is disgusting." Ethan swiped his hair off his forehead with one shirtsleeve. Sweat glistened on his hairline.

Sam couldn't help the bubble of satisfaction fizzing in her stomach. She leaned back against the stall wall and let it hold her weight. Served Ethan right. If ranching was so easy, every city slicker would hustle down from the North and give it a whirl. Ethan deserved a good dose of reality. And if that came by pitchfork and manure, then all the better.

"You do this for every stall in the barn?" Ethan dropped a load from his pitchfork into the wheelbarrow and wrinkled his nose.

"Every single day. Cole helps, usually. But this morning I told him we'd handle it." Sam grinned.

"We?" Ethan stopped shoveling and stared, resting one arm atop the long wooden handle of the fork. "You've done nothing but point."

"Hey, you're the one who wanted to learn about ranching." Sam adjusted the rim of her cowboy hat in an exaggerated air of indifference. "I'm just trying to help."

"Quit the sarcasm. It's too early in the morning." He went back to scooping, watching Piper as warily as Piper watched him. "Couldn't you have taken her out of the stall for this?"

"Him. And there's no reason to. He only uses this one corner."

"Who teaches them that?"

"It's a natural instinct that most animals have." Sam watched Ethan work a moment longer, than sighed. "All right, fine. I'll shovel the next one." She didn't feel guilty, exactly—just wasn't used to standing around without purpose. She reached for the pitchfork.

"No way. I asked for this, remember?" Ethan refused to relinquish the handle.

She tugged back on it. "I can manage—apparently better than you can."

"What's that supposed to mean?" He pulled harder.

"It means I'm used to hard work."

"And I'm not?" Ethan's expression tightened.

Sam gripped the handle with both hands. "I didn't say that."

"But you thought it." Ethan let go and Sam stumbled backward several steps. "You sure do lose your balance a lot."

She quickly regained her stance and pointed the pitchfork at him. "At least I'm not afraid to try."

"Look, I know what you're thinking." Ethan waved both hands in the air. "The rich city boy never had to do anything but learn how to feed himself with a silver spoon. Right?"

Sam opened her mouth, then snapped it shut. He was dead-on—and why should she think differently? He flaunted his self-importance. Kate had warned her the Ameses' first day at the ranch to watch out for tourists. She'd been joking, of course, but Sam would be better off taking the remark seriously. Ethan was the exact image of the stereotypical, heartless guy, searching for a new hobby that he would inevitably tire of. But what if he tired of it before his vacation ended and broke his end of their deal? Angie would be devastated, Sam would have to quit the competition, and there went any chance of buying Noble Star or bringing back the breeding business. Sam's home would forever be a tourist trap.

No, as much as she wanted to throw the pitchfork at Ethan and walk away, she had to keep him happy. There was too much at stake. She gritted her teeth. "Why don't we start over?"

"With the stall?" Ethan's eyes widened in alarm.

"No, not with mucking out the stable. With us. With this." She gestured between them.

"What's the catch?" Ethan's caramel-brown gaze turned cautious.

Sam rested the pitchfork against the gate. "No catch. I just think if we're going to be around each other, the least we can do is be civil about it."

"Civil, as in, no more sarcasm?"

"I make no promises." The corners of Sam's mouth twitched into a grin.

Ethan's eyes shimmered in amusement as he held out his hand. "Fair enough. Truce?"

"Truce." Sam slipped her palm against his and a spark ignited at contact. She quickly pulled it back, wondering if he felt it, too. From the way Ethan wrung his hand once before reaching to pick up the wheelbarrow, she could only assume he had.

"Which way?" He gripped the handles and maneuvered the full barrow toward the door.

Sam opened the gate and pointed toward the far end of the barn. "Outside and to the right is a compost pile. You can't miss it."

Ethan squeezed past Sam through the opening. The lingering look he shot over his shoulder before he headed down the barn aisle made her breath hitch.

Sam secured the gate and paused a moment to give Ethan a much-needed head start.

Couldn't miss it, indeed.

Never in his life had Ethan imagined he'd be dumping horse manure into a compost pile. Even more than that, he had never imagined he'd be doing it with a ridiculous smile on his face that wouldn't quit. Good thing Sam stayed in the barn or else she'd think he was nuts.

Ethan turned the empty wheelbarrow away from the compost pile and back toward the stable. That electric spark he felt when Sam shook his hand wasn't imaginary—it was real. Which meant he was either losing his mind—or falling for the enemy. His dad would panic for sure if he knew Ethan had felt something, really felt something, at that contact.

Truce. He snorted. Making that kind of agreement with Sam was more dangerous than continuing the sarcastic battle of wills they'd had before. He'd much rather shoot barbs than sparks.

Ethan straightened his shoulders as he pushed the wheelbarrow down the stable aisle. It didn't matter whether Sam's touch made his entire arm feel as if he'd been struck by light-ning. It didn't matter if she was intriguing, sweet and spicy all at the same time. It didn't matter, because she was an obstacle, the barrier to navigate on the way to his dreams. If he'd learned anything worthwhile from Jeffrey Ames, it was that goals on the road of life were never reached by stopping to pick wildflowers along the way.

Ethan cracked his neck in one quick motion and schooled his features as he handed over the wheelbarrow handles to Sam. Her eyes, wide and luminous beneath the brim of her hat, made his stomach flip—eyes the exact color of the periwinkle wildflowers in the meadow behind the barn. He drew a steadying breath. This was ridiculous. He was Ethan Ames. No way would he be bested by some tomboy in boots.

Even if she had him thinking about wildflowers.

Chapter Eight

Sam shut the dishwasher with a clank and turned it on. She straightened, pressing her hands into the small of her back. Nothing worse than completing a day of outside chores just to come in and work equally hard in the kitchen. But she'd taken one look at Clara buried under a mountain of dishes, and couldn't let the older woman handle it by herself. Besides, Angie was paying bills in the computer nook off the den, and the kitchen was the farthest room away from the bitter mutterings and frustrated pen clicks.

Clara tossed a sponge in the sink and untied her apron from around her ample waist. "I think that does it. Thank you for helping me with the dishes."

"No problem. After that meal, how could I let you do them alone?" Sam patted her stomach with a smile. "Good thing I work so hard, huh? I think I had three helpings of mashed potatoes."

Clara tsked as she hung her apron on a peg by the industrial-sized refrigerator. "You could stand a few more pounds, if you asked me. I've never seen such skinny women like you and your mother."

"We burn a lot of calories."

"Ain't right for a woman to be skin and bones." Clara winked as she shouldered her purse and draped her navy sweater over one arm. "I'll fatten you both up yet."

"I have no problem letting you try." Sam patted Clara on the arm as she walked with her to the door. "Thanks again for the pot roast."

"Just doing my job. You all have a good night." Clara shut the door behind her and once again, the Jenson household was silent.

Sam turned off the kitchen light and released a heavy sigh. She needed a hot bath—would maybe even throw some bubbles, a book and a soda into the mix. Working so hard every day did have at least one silver lining—Sam had basically become immune to caffeine. She could drink coffee in bed if she wanted and still sleep soundly.

She wiped her tired eyes with the back of her hand. On second thought, maybe she'd skip the bath and the drink and head straight to her room. She could use a solid eight hours of sleep—too bad she'd only get three at best before having to sneak out for her midnight ride with Cole and Lucy. Maybe this time Ethan wouldn't crash the practice session. Even with Ethan shadowing her around the stable all day, Sam had still successfully avoided telling him why she was determined to ride the steer in the first place. That was one more complication she just didn't need.

Sam tiptoed past the computer nook. Hopefully her mom wouldn't hear her on that squeaky bottom step—

"Sam? Is that you?" Angie's voice sounded more exhausted than Sam felt.

Sam hesitated on the staircase. Then guilt took precedence over exhaustion and she shuffled into the den. "How's it going?"

"Same as always." Angie pushed her short, sandy-colored hair back from her face. The light from the desk lamp shone on her tanned skin and she rested her elbows on the tabletop.

Sam swallowed the pride lingering in her throat and forced the words she'd hoped to never utter from her mouth. "Do you need me to get a second job again?" She held her breath.

Angie sighed. "That's thoughtful, but we'd be worse off losing the work you do around here."

Relief crowded Sam's already full stomach. She couldn't handle an outside job, not among her other daily chores on the ranch and her new hours of training for the upcoming competition.

Sam studied her mother's scribbled notes in the margins of the ledger book. If only she could tell her mom her plan to save the ranch she would, but the timing was more than a little off. As soon as Angie heard the words *bull* and *rodeo,* she'd go berserk—even under the best of circumstances. Bill paying was probably the worst timing of all. Until Sam was positive her mom would understand that the end result was well worth the risk, she'd have to stick to her original plan of keeping the secret. Sam peered over her mom's shoulder to better read the bottom line. "Are we going to be okay?"

"We'll make it." Angie shoved up the sleeves of her shirt and bent over the pile of envelopes and the ledger book, shielding it from Sam's view. "We always do, somehow. But if we considered selling..."

"Things will get better soon." The promise rolled off Sam's tongue before she could stop it, desperate to ease the stress lines tainting Angie's once-young face. Sam hoped she'd be able to make the assurance true and keep the farm where it belonged—with the Jensons.

"I know. God always provides, doesn't He? Your optimism

is contagious." Angie's smile appeared slightly more sincere this time and she squeezed Sam's hand. "Go to bed. You've done enough for tonight."

Sam squeezed back before turning and heading silently up the stairs to her room. She hadn't done anything yet, not anything that mattered, at least—but she was about to, starting with round two on Lucy.

Would it be enough?

Ethan's muscles ached, his head throbbed, and his eyes felt sticky from lack of sleep—yet he'd never felt so good in his life. Who knew hard manual labor carried even more endorphins than his logged treadmill miles?

He glanced at the digital alarm clock on the nightstand. Only fifteen minutes until Sam would be at the north paddock with Cole and that crazy bull—no, steer. The scariest part of the whole experience was that he hadn't minded the chores nearly as much as he'd expected. Mucking out the stables wasn't exactly fun—especially after the sparks with Sam when they touched hands—but grooming the horses, learning how to saddle them for trail rides, and helping distribute fresh hay to all the stalls hadn't been bad. Pleasant, even, once he and Sam kept to their no-more-arguing truce.

Now if only his emotions could stick to the pact he made with himself.

Ethan tapped his watch with his finger. Ten minutes until practice time. He hadn't told Sam he was coming, but it should be assumed. They were in it together. He just still didn't know what this "it" was. Sam had yet to tell him why she was on that steer last night—a fact Ethan planned to remedy in a few short minutes.

He eased out of bed and slipped into his running shoes,

careful not to disturb Daniel. His cousin had returned to the cabin earlier in the evening, griping about how the girls he'd been flirting with earlier in the week had already gone back home, their vacation over. Daniel had crashed in his bed and immediately started snoring.

Ethan shook his head at Daniel's sleeping form and crept out the front door, wincing at the loud click. He waited, but Daniel didn't make a sound from inside. With a relieved sigh, he turned—and bumped straight into Jeffrey's broad chest.

"Dad!" Ethan gulped, hoping his surprise didn't show on his face. To Jeffrey Ames, being unprepared was an indicator of weakness. No matter that his dad was skulking around the cabin porch in the dark—it'd still be Ethan's fault for being startled. He straightened his shoulders and lowered his voice. "What are you doing?"

"Coming to wake you up to talk." Jeffrey gripped Ethan's elbow and led him down the stairs and around the corner of the cabin. The grass squished under their shoes. "What progress have you made with the Jenson girl?"

"Sam?" Ethan's heart raced and again, he hoped his dad wouldn't notice. He'd definitely have to work on his poker face when it came to Sam—at least until logic overtook his emotions.

"Sam, Pam, whatever. I haven't seen you all day. What do you know? What have you been doing?" Jeffrey crossed his arms.

Ethan recognized the pose—the businesslike, get-it-done posture that Jeffrey took on regardless of the cost. His dad wanted answers, and he wanted them now. "I've been with Sam all day. Like you wanted me to be."

"Has she mentioned anything that could be useful for our cause?"

Ethan winced, remembering the ignited handshake in the barn, Sam's melodic laugh and the way his eyes stayed drawn to her all day as if they'd been taken over by a magnetic force. "Not yet."

"Well, you need to step it up. We're running out of time."

"Already? We've only been here three days."

Jeffrey shook his head impatiently. "Business waits for no man, you know that. Your mother is afraid Ms. Jenson will hear about that highway relocation before we can make our offer. If she does, she's more likely to discover our intentions of building the strip mall—and then she'd never sell to us. We're having enough trouble convincing her to sell under the pretense of keeping the property exactly as it is. We have to move fast—before Sam realizes why we're here, and before Ms. Jenson decides not to take an offer. She's wavering because of her daughter." Jeffrey scoffed. "Something about so many memories here."

"What do you want me to do? I can't make up reasons to offer less money." Ethan quickly replayed the events of the past two days for his father, omitting the details of Sam's secret riding plans. No use in sharing private, personal matters with Jeffrey. The man didn't have a personal bone in his body. "Maybe we should just offer them a fair price. We'd still make money off the deal when the highway comes."

"Are you crazy? After spending time on this ramshackle place, the last thing I'm going to do is offer more money." Jeffrey brushed at his forehead and the moonlight caught in the reflective face of his watch. "We're going to have to go a step further."

"What now? You want me to date Sam instead of just trying to be her friend?" Some tiny, twisted part of Ethan's psyche hoped his father would say yes. Not that Sam would ever agree. She probably only fell for real cowboys—men who smelled like sweat and earth instead of expensive cologne.

Ethan brushed away the pinch of rejection at the idea. This was business. He didn't need romance.

Especially with a woman with eyes like periwinkle wildflowers.

"Don't be ridiculous." Jeffrey's harsh laugh jerked Ethan back to the conversation. "If I wanted someone to romance the girl, I'd ask Daniel." He scoffed and Ethan tried to ignore the way the barb pierced the same, worn dent in his emotional armor. "Maybe you can find proof that the ranch is failing, specific proof. If she has to sell, she won't worry as much about her daughter's feelings."

"What if there isn't any?" Ethan adjusted his stance to mirror his dad's.

"Then make some."

Ethan flinched.

"Keep on befriending the girl. She needs to trust you." Jeffrey looked over his shoulder and lowered his gruff voice to a near whisper. "But in the meantime, look for ways to sabotage the property. Cut fences. Destroy feed. Poison it, for all I care. We need Angie to accept our offer, and we need her to do it now."

Ethan's stomach twisted. He could never purposefully hurt any of the horses, or Sam. Besides, Ethan *wanted* to be near her—and not just because he was ordered to for his job. He opened his mouth to object.

Jeffrey caught Ethan's shoulder in one large hand and bent down to his level. "Do it, or I'll get your cousin to handle things for you." He straightened, lowering his hand to his side, but the weight of it continued to rest on Ethan's shoulders. "It's your choice."

Jeffrey turned and strode back to his cabin, his back ramrod straight in the lengthening shadows. Ethan trudged in the opposite direction toward the north paddock, the excitement of seeing Sam suddenly ruined. He spun his father's words over and over in his mind, the meaning striking with new clarity at each rotation. *It's your choice.*

None of this was Ethan's choice. That was the whole problem in the first place. Ethan didn't get to choose his career. He didn't get to choose how he did his job, or which bank to use or even which college to attend. He had no choices at all. But there was no way he'd allow his father or Daniel to sabotage Sam's ranch.

Ethan's eyes narrowed at Jeffrey's retreating form, growing smaller the more distance he put between them. He'd show his father about choices, all right.

Starting with Sam.

Chapter Nine

The next morning, Sam jerked the cinch strap and adjusted the saddle pad on Diego's back. Then she looped the reins over the fence post, grabbed Piper's blanket from the top paddock rail and moved toward the gelding waiting on the other side of Diego. At least the chestnut's ankle had finally completely healed.

She blew an annoying strand of hair out of her eyes as she slid the checkered blanket over Piper's sweaty back. It seemed like every guest on the ranch had showed up for the Tuesday morning ride and was waiting impatiently for a horse—even the honeymoon couple. She and Cole had their hands full trying to get the animals ready, and the sun already shone hot on Sam's head. A fly buzzed by Piper's mane and she swatted it. Thankfully, the wind was blowing, a welcome respite from the July heat.

"Miss Priss is ready." Cole patted the mare's cheek as he ducked under her neck. "I'll start helping the riders mount."

"Thanks, Cole." Sam yawned and noted the matching fatigue shadowing Cole's face. She pushed aside a wave of guilt. She might owe Cole for helping her practice in the middle of the night, but the end result would benefit the generous stable hand, too. They'd both be free from the guests, the endless questions, and the commercialization of the only home they'd known—although at this point, they were also both in danger of falling asleep in the saddle.

"Mornin', partner." Ethan's exaggerated cowboy drawl sounded over Sam's shoulder and she couldn't help but smile. Ethan had watched her practice session last night on the steer, and she didn't know what was more amusing—her own efforts to stay on Lucy's back or the look on Ethan's face every time Sam fell off. If panic had a tangible form, Ethan would have been wearing it.

Sam handed Piper's reins to Cole so he could lead the gelding to a guest. She turned to Ethan, the wind whipping her hair in front of her eyes. "Is the rest of your family joining you for the ride?"

"My mom probably will, as long as she's nowhere near Piper again." Ethan laughed. "Do you have a deaf horse?"

"Very funny." Sam glanced over her shoulder as Vickie Ames strode into the mounting area in a stark white button-down and jeans. That shirt probably wouldn't stay pristine for long, but if the Ames family were as wealthy as Sam's mother kept hinting, Vickie could easily get another ensemble. She could probably fully outfit every rider on the ranch for their entire vacation and never even notice the expense. What did the Ames family do that they were so successful with? She should ask Ethan about his career. Not that it really mattered—the knowledge wouldn't change the dwindling dollars in the Jensons' checking account.

Sam's mood darkened as she took Miss Priss's reins and strode toward the start of the trail where the others waited. What would it be like to have that kind of money? Ethan and his family had never wanted for a thing, while Sam and her mother struggled just to pay the electric bill and the gas bill in the same month.

"Are you okay?" Ethan caught up to Sam and touched her shoulder. "You walked off pretty fast."

She eased away from the innocent contact, too upset to care how the touch held just as much spark as it had yesterday in the barn. Fireworks were dangerous, and so was Ethan Ames. She forced a smile. "Fine. Just busy."

"Can I help? Partner?" Ethan smiled.

Sam winced at the teamwork reference. She should have never made a bargain with Ethan, though she supposed it was better than the alternative of him blabbing her secret to her mom. It wasn't his fault that he had money and a successful family business. There was no reason to take her anger out on him.

She blew out her breath and fought for control of her exhausted emotions. "I think Cole and I have it under control. Looks like you're riding Miss Priss again." She handed Ethan the reins, careful to avoid brushing his fingers in the process, and strode toward Diego. Ethan's gaze burned into her back the entire way.

Sam and Ethan might be forced together for the time being, but she didn't have to like it—didn't have to like him. He was on vacation, and while it was nice having the extra help for the chores yesterday, Ethan was bound to get bored soon. And once he did, the workload would fall once again on Sam's weary shoulders, along with everything else that had taken permanent residence there.

She gripped the saddle horn in one hand and easily swung onto Diego's back, automatically dropping her heels and squeezing with her lower legs to urge him toward the rest of the group.

It was a wonder the poor gelding didn't collapse from the weight of all the problems Sam bore.

* * *

Ethan couldn't stop staring at the back of Sam's head. At least this time on the trail, he felt somewhat more comfortable in the saddle, and could afford the time spent thinking now that he wasn't worrying about falling off. His upper body swayed in rhythm to Miss Priss's smooth steps as the sun warmed the tops of his shoulders. What was Sam's problem? She'd smiled like she was happy to see him, then turned distant so fast he'd almost gotten whiplash.

He adjusted his hands on the reins, ducking along with the rest of the string of riders as they cleared a low-hanging branch. *Women.* Changing their moods more often than Daniel changed his socks. But Sam didn't seem the type to play the same mind games that the women he was accustomed to often did. Something specific must have happened to douse her spirits during those few minutes in the paddock.

Only one way to find out what. Ethan clucked to his horse as he'd seen Sam do and sidled the mare up to the front of the line, next to Sam. Her eyes widened beneath her cowboy hat and she slowed Diego's pace to match Miss Priss's. "Is something wrong? Is it your mom?"

"No, she's fine. I just wanted to talk." Ethan glanced at the trail ahead of them. Plenty of room for two horses to walk side by side, so she'd have no reason to avoid talking to him. "Are you feeling all right?"

"I'm fine." Sam faced forward again, her expression stony.

"Are you mad that I wasn't at the stable this morning? I meant to be, but I forgot to set the alarm after the late night."

"It's okay. You're on vacation. You shouldn't be working in the first place." Sam's shoulders tensed and Diego tossed his head, pulling against the reins.

"We have a deal, remember? I don't mind working. I asked

to." His father's manipulative plan pressed on Ethan's conscience, and he shifted in the saddle. He should tell Sam the truth about why his family was there. But then she'd never talk to him again. Plus, if he backed out of his father's schemes now, he'd be outside the loop and would have no idea what his family was plotting against Sam and her mom. How could he protect her if he was cut off from the information?

Ethan cleared his throat. "Really, I don't mind the chores. I like learning about the ranch."

"Why?" Sam turned toward him so fast Ethan wondered how she didn't fall off Diego's back. "Why do you care so much?"

Ethan's mouth opened, then closed. "I guess if you get to keep your secret about why you're riding a steer, then I get to keep mine." He smiled, and Sam's lips turned up at the corners before she schooled her features back into stone.

"Fine. Be stubborn." She nudged Diego with her knees and pulled ahead.

Ethan tapped Miss Priss's sides with his heels and caught up. "About your riding that steer—" His voice broke off as Sam edged ahead once again. He pressed forward. "Listen, I'm serious. You don't have to tell me why if you don't want to, but whatever the reason, isn't there a better way? It seems dangerous. You fell a lot, and those horns—"

Diego stopped suddenly and Sam's eyes flashed with fire. Ethan reeled backward at the burn. "Don't you dare pretend to understand me." An almost tangible tension filtered through her tight-lipped words.

"I don't." Ethan shook his head to clear the shock residue. Of all the women in the entire world, Sam was probably the least predictable and easy to understand—and he'd been to a lot of places.

"There isn't another way. Trust me." Sam urged Diego into a walk. "You wouldn't get it."

Ethan followed. "You're trusting me with your secret in general—so why not the details of it?"

Sam's jaw clenched and she looked away.

Ethan waited, but didn't push. He was already threatening their delicate truce, but Sam didn't realize Ethan was doing her a favor by not following his dad's orders to sabotage the ranch. She had no idea what was at stake, and the more Ethan knew, the better he could protect Sam from his father's manipulation—and try to reach his own goals without picking wildflowers along the way.

Sam avoided his eyes. "It's not a matter of trust, Ethan. You forced this deal."

Guilt pricked Ethan's heart like a tailor's pin. "For good reason."

"A reason you're going to share?" The silence between them pulsed heavy with expectation.

"I just wanted to spend time with yo—just wanted to learn about working a ranch, and I knew you'd never agree without some kind of extra motivation." Ethan shook his head at the near slip. He *had* wanted to spend time with Sam, and not just because his dad insisted—but because Ethan wanted to be around her, wanted to soak in her presence like a much needed rain shower.

"I find it hard to believe you're actually interested in cleaning stalls and grooming horses." Sam's eyebrows rose and her face shadowed under the brim of her hat.

"But I am." Again, it was the truth. There was something rewarding about rising early and working with his hands, not just pushing papers around on a mahogany desk while staring at the view from his twentieth-floor, high-rise condo. "Sam, please. Just tell me what's going on."

She tossed her hair, the sun highlighting the honey strands brushing across her back, and inhaled deeply. "I need money, and there's a bull-riding rodeo competition in a little over a week."

"Why do you need money?" What could be so important that she'd risk her life? Was the ranch struggling that badly? At that point, Ethan and his family had less "work" to do than they'd thought, but right now he only cared about finding a way to make Sam smile again.

Sam looked over her shoulder, and Ethan's head automatically swiveled with hers. The rest of the riders in their group were several paces back, talking and gesturing at the meadow view to their left. Sam turned back to Ethan, apparently satisfied no one was listening. "My best friend's father is selling a stallion. Noble Star could help my family resurrect our old breeding business."

Ethan's lips pressed together. Sam was entering the rodeo to win a horse. How could one stallion make or break an entire business? He still didn't get why Sam felt compelled to ride a steer—a bull—when there were more conventional options of obtaining money. "What about a loan?"

"Not possible."

The firm set of Sam's jaw convinced Ethan not to force that route. Sam was a smart woman—if there was a way to get money from a bank, she'd have done it by now. There were probably credit issues involved, and logically so considering the state of the ranch and his own family's presence. "Why not sell the stallions in that fence by the guest cabins? They're not being used anymore, are they?"

"Not for guests. Cole and I still work them regularly to keep them exercised. But if we sold them and were able to start the breeding farm again, then we'd have nothing to start with. They could still earn us some money, but it'd be too time-consuming to get off the ground without a head start like Noble Star." Sam shrugged. "Not to mention we have zero free time right now running the dude ranch business."

"Is the dude ranch not bringing in enough income?"

"It pays the bills. Barely." Sam shifted her weight in the saddle, the brushed leather creaking beneath her. "But this isn't what it should be. This isn't home anymore." Sam leaned forward to pat Diego's neck, but not before Ethan saw a single tear track her cheek.

He let the silence protect her misery, and waited until she wiped her face and cleared her throat. Then he smiled. "I'm sure if anyone can meet their goals, Sam, it's you."

He'd always been a sucker for wildflowers.

Chapter Ten

Sprawled on packed dirt, staring up at the stars dotting the inky black sky, Sam wondered if this whole brilliant plan of hers was worth it. Divine providence, or just a really stupid mistake? She pushed herself into a sitting position and brushed at her dusty sleeves, ignoring Cole's amused grin, Ethan's furrowed brow and the throbbing of her right shoulder. At least Kate's expression was one of sympathy and respect.

"Need a hand?" Cole called from the chute. He grabbed the rope around Lucy's girth and began freeing the steer.

"No." Sam stood on her own, despite the soreness. What she really needed was a stun gun, one to point first at Lucy, and then at Ethan. If he didn't knock off that parental worry he wore on his face like a permanent mask, she'd clobber him. It was bad enough having Cole treat her like she was made of china, another for Ethan to watch and cringe as if she would break. Why did he care so much? Ethan barely knew her, and yet his tenderness earlier in the day on the trail ride tugged at Sam's heart. It'd been a vulnerable moment on her part, moments that grew rarer and rarer the busier Sam stayed, and she could have kicked herself for crying in front of Ethan. The stress of the past few weeks—make that years—had gotten to her. It figured her weakness would bloom in front of a guest—one with chocolate-brown eyes and a smile that beckoned, despite the warnings screaming in Sam's mind.

Avoiding Ethan's gaze, Sam turned to Cole. "How long that time?"

Cole checked the stopwatch he held between calloused fingers. "Four seconds. And that's giving you a tenth."

Kate clapped her hands. "Not bad!"

"More like awful." Sam groaned. "This isn't working. Lucy isn't even a real bull, and I can't manage."

Cole pocketed the watch. "You can't expect to be a pro after a few days of practice, kid."

Kate shook her red curls back from her face. "Yeah, Sam. It takes time. But you've made amazing progress."

"I don't *have* time." Sam pressed her fingers against her forehead. No time, no money, no patience. Nothing but a big balloon of stress pressing against her temples. "I might as well be a rodeo clown. I'm a joke."

Ethan straightened from his slumped position against the fence beside Kate. "No, you're not. That's ridiculous."

She briefly squeezed her eyes shut. "What's ridiculous is me riding Lucy." Sam had gotten in over her head—and now was sinking faster than a baby calf in quicksand. Good intentions didn't hold nearly as much merit when she was on the ground staring up at the horned beast. At least her father wasn't here to see her failure. Tears burned the back of Sam's throat.

"Nothing is ridiculous. You just expect too much of yourself." Cole tossed the rope over the fence and slapped Lucy's rump. The steer ambled out of the chute and began nibbling at the grass growing through the rail.

They really should hedge around the posts, the weeds were practically inside the paddock. Though if the grass kept growing inside the fence, it'd just be extra padding to land on when flying off Lucy. Sam swallowed back a rush of overwhelming emotion. Would the to-do list around the ranch ever be caught up? Not without money. Not without Noble Star. She groaned. If only Kate's father could lower the price of the stallion. But even if he would, could she accept charity like that? She and her mom had made it on their own this long, even if they were a little worse for the wear because of it. She couldn't let someone else pave the way now, even if that meant she had to take the bull by the horns—literally.

Ethan climbed on the top of the fence and hesitated, as if he wasn't sure he wanted to jump to the ground on the other side or not. "Look, I'm sure there's a better way for you to get money than this whole bull-riding thing." He wobbled, and grabbed the rail with both hands.

"And I'm sure in *your* world, there's plenty of ways." Sam glared. "But welcome to reality."

Cole cocked his head to one side and crossed his arms. "Why is this guy still here, anyway? You want me to get rid of him?" He directed the question to Sam but stared at Ethan. Ethan shifted again on the fence and nearly toppled off. Kate shot out her arm to steady him and grinned at Ethan's responding scowl.

"It's a long story." *Too long.* Sam tucked her hair behind both ears and sighed.

Cole shook his head as he began coiling the rope. "Seems to me your list of debtors is getting longer every day, kid."

"Sam, seriously, you can find other ways to earn money." Ethan landed awkwardly on his feet inside the pen. "This is crazy. Let me help you."

"This is not crazy. My dad did it." A rapidly fraying thread inside Sam snapped and fresh tears added to the pressure pounding in her head. She jerked away from Ethan's outstretched hand. "And I don't take charity."

"I'm not talking about charity." Ethan looked at Cole, as if for help.

The cowboy's features tightened, and Sam welcomed the rush of warmth that Cole's protection offered. At least someone was looking out for her. Her surrogate big brother believed in Sam's riding ability, so who cared if a near-stranger did not? The flippant thought tugged at Sam's stomach. She did care what Ethan thought, more than she had the strength to acknowledge.

Kate quickly climbed the fence—much smoother than Ethan had—and looped her arm around Sam's shoulders. "Maybe Ethan has a point. We should try to come up with another plan. I don't want you to get hurt."

Flashbacks of hooves, horns and hospital beds filled Sam's mind and she blinked against the torrent. She didn't want to get hurt, either. But if a simple bake sale or car wash could solve the farm's problems, Sam would have been whipping up cupcakes and lathering trucks long ago. It wasn't as if she had a long list of options. She sank against the fence. "It's not that easy."

"It can be if you get creative." Ethan stepped beside her.

A frown crinkled Kate's eyebrows. "Sam, do you really want to do this? Is it that important to you? If it is, we'll support you. Or at least I will." She shot a wary look at Ethan.

Ethan's eyes narrowed. "It's not a matter of being supportive. I just don't want Sam to end up under some bull's hooves."

The audible blow landed like a sledgehammer to Sam's heart. She gasped in pain and Cole's face darkened. "Drop it,

Ames. You don't know what you're talking about." Without waiting for a reply, Cole grabbed Lucy's rope and led her toward the barn, his boots clomping loudly on the packed dirt. The shadows swallowed them whole as they disappeared inside the stable.

"Was it something I said?" Ethan winced.

Kate's eyes bugged. "You mean, you don't know?"

Sam quickly interrupted. "Kate, it's okay." Ethan didn't know the details of her father's death, or else he'd probably have used better terms. But she wasn't ready to tell him—not now, maybe not ever. Sam drew a shuddery breath. If that look on Cole's face had been any indication, he'd felt the sting of Ethan's unintentional barb, too. Sometimes Sam forgot she wasn't the only one hurt when Wade Jenson died. He'd been like an uncle to Cole.

Kate's lips pressed together and she nodded in understanding. "I'm gonna take off, then. I'll call you tomorrow." She glanced at Ethan, shook her head and made her way silently toward her pickup parked across the field.

"So is Cole just your spokesman?" Ethan leaned his elbow against the rail beside Sam. A strand of dark hair, long ago having lost its gel, sagged against his forehead. "Or something more?"

Sam turned to face the same direction, lodging one booted foot against the bottom rail. "He's more like a big brother than anything else. He watched me grow up."

"Stable hand by day, protector by night."

"Something like that." Sam tossed back her hair. "But I speak for myself." She always had, after her father died. If she didn't, no one would.

The breeze stirred Ethan's hair and puffed the sleeves of his polo shirt. At least he hadn't resorted to wearing those designer shirts with the pearl buttons that Daniel wore. He must have thirty of those things and changed them twice a day. Sam wasn't sure what was more annoying—that Daniel was trying too hard to fit into the ranch world, making a mockery of it in the process—or that Ethan fit in without seemingly trying at all. He simply did the work like any other stable hand, minus the traditional attire. Hard as she tried, Sam couldn't picture Ethan in anything other than his signature jeans, khakis or polo.

Although a black felt cowboy hat would really bring out his mysterious dark eyes.

Sam jerked, stung by the errant thought, and slid away from the fence. "I've got to go. It's late."

"If I said something to hurt you, I'm sorry." Ethan's quiet voice broke the silence of the night.

"It's not your fault." In a way she wished it was. Then she could channel the anger and frustration toward someone, toward something tangible. But she had no one to blame for her and her mother's current situation. It wasn't her father's fault, and Sam knew better than to blame God—completely, anyway. His grace had been the only thing to get them through the blindingly dark days after Wade's death. Maybe riding that bull would be the therapy she needed. Not only would it accomplish her goal for the farm, but it could release the years of buried tension. Is that why her dad rode all those years?

Too much to think about on sore muscles and no sleep.

"I'll see you tomorrow." She lifted her hand in a wave to Ethan and quickly slipped away toward the main house, toward the solace of her bedroom, toward precious sleep that could numb the emotion for another night.

Toward the pillow she'd already sobbed into enough for one lifetime.

* * *

Ethan watched Sam walk away from him, and not for the first time. He thought he'd found the perfect opportunity to talk Sam out of this crazy bull-riding idea and into something tamer. But she seemed determined to do this, and for reasons he hadn't yet grasped. How many more secrets were hovering over the Jenson ranch?

Ethan gripped the paddock fence with both hands and winced at a splinter that worked its way under his skin. Sort of like a certain cowgirl. He'd known Sam for, what, a week or less? And he was already overly concerned about her well-being—his heart pounding every time the steer bucked, his stomach tightening every time Sam fell. This was foolish. It was a crush, at best. Sam was different from the women he was used to dating, so she seemed appealing. That was all, right? Opposites might attract, but they rarely meshed. It'd be stupid of him to think otherwise.

He shoved away from the fence and headed toward his cabin, the lie stinging worse than the splinter in his palm. He didn't need this. He was here to make a sale, gain financial independence and hit the road. Figuratively and literally. Sam was a distraction—a beautiful one, but still a distraction. He had to find a way to get this whole business scheme of his father's over with before he did something stupid.

Like fall in love.

There was a note scribbled on Ethan's nightstand informing him that Daniel couldn't sleep and had gone to play pool in the lodge. He wanted Ethan to come meet him when he got back from his date. Ethan's lip curled as he tossed the letter in the trash. Watching Sam get trounced by a beast wasn't a date, and definitely not with that Cole guy watching his every move.

Ethan stood in the middle of the room, halfway between

his bed and the door. He could go put up with Daniel and his competitive streak, or he could go to bed.

And dream about Sam all night.

With a scowl, Ethan yanked the door open and shouldered through the cool night air toward the lodge. At least he could be certain Sam went to her home to sleep and not to the big game room off the main house.

Daniel waved from the back corner of the room and tossed him a stick. "Glad you made it. Now I can beat someone instead of playing by myself." He broke and the balls scattered across the green felt. "Stripes." He missed the next one.

"Nice try. You're going down." Ethan leaned over the table and lined up his shot, eager to vent his frustration. The cue ball ricocheted off a solid orange and slid easily into a corner pocket.

Daniel grunted his approval. "So where were you tonight? And don't give me that meeting junk again."

"It was a meeting."

"Right. And I'm Annie Oakley."

Ethan aimed for the solid green and overshot. "Your turn."

"You didn't answer me." Daniel sunk a striped ball in the left corner. "You were with Sam."

"It was work-related."

"I'd like to work with her." Daniel winked as he studied the table for an opening.

Ethan gripped the cue stick with both hands. He knew Daniel would try to weasel into his relationship with Sam, had seen it coming a mile away. Ethan blinked. Wait a minute. What relationship? He shook his head. This entire process was getting too confusing. One thing he knew for sure, he didn't want his womanizing cousin anywhere near Sam.

Daniel powered another ball into the hole. "Is she seeing anyone?"

"I don't think so." He'd never asked, but there was no way Sam had time for dating. It was obvious her focus remained solidly on the ranch and her goals. Ethan cleared his throat. "But she's not your type."

"I like all types."

"Just leave her alone." Ethan's voice rose and he quickly bit his lip. But it was too late. The truth glimmered in Daniel's eyes and he grinned.

"No problem, man. You can have her. I won't give you any competition, even if your dad did ask me to."

Disbelief clouded Ethan's vision. His father had just said the other night that he didn't want Ethan getting close to Sam romantically. In fact, Jeffrey's exact words were *Don't be ridiculous, if I wanted someone to date Sam, I'd ask Daniel.*

Reality struck hard and Ethan's heart stammered. His dad was manipulating them all. It was so obvious now. If Jeffrey could ask Ethan to lie, then he wouldn't have any problem lying in return—even to his family.

Daniel leaned over, aimed and sunk the eight ball into the corner. "That's the game."

Ethan swallowed the mixture of anger, embarrassment and denial rising in his throat as he returned the cue stick to its stand by the wall.

It was a game, all right.

Chapter Eleven

"You didn't have to come." Sam shot a sidelong glance at Ethan, who ambled along beside her on Miss Priss. A breeze chilled the morning heat on Sam's back. Even Diego's withers felt warm under her fingers. Just another typical July day in Appleback, Texas. She pushed at the cowboy hat on her head, knowing her hair must be a sweaty mess underneath. "You could have gone with Cole and the others on the regular ride."

"Checking fences is part of ranch life, isn't it?" Ethan grinned and the sun highlighted his brown hair. "I want to learn it all."

"It might get boring."

"I doubt that." Ethan's eyes held a deeper meaning and Sam quickly looked away, her heart stuttering.

Beneath her, Diego stirred and Sam tried to calm the rush of emotion her mount noticed. "Better you than Ethan," she mumbled to the horse.

Ethan leaned over in the saddle. "What's that?"

"Nothing." Sam smiled, hoping it covered the confusion she knew lingered in her eyes. She squeezed Diego's side to urge him into a trot. "Let's go. At this rate, we'll never finish checking the borders."

They rode toward the east perimeter, the weeds and overgrown grass parting around the horses' legs. Ethan didn't bounce nearly as hard in the saddle as he did on their first trail ride, and Sam shoved back the smidgen of pride for her part in the improvement. She might be a good teacher but Ethan, as much as she hated to admit it, had natural ability on a horse. He just needed the time and confidence—which he was obviously gaining as he no longer clung to the saddle horn—to develop it.

"What happens if we find a break in the fence?" Ethan's eager expression seemed as if he hoped they would.

"We note it and send Cole back later to fix it."

"You can't fix it yourself?" Ethan's cocked eyebrow held a challenge, and Sam bristled.

"Of course I *could.* But it's barbed wire and Cole's stronger. He can pull it three times as fast as me." Not to mention she hated messing with those sharp barbs. Besides, it wasn't like she didn't already have enough on her cracked, overflowing plate. "Time is money on a farm."

Ethan's mouth twitched.

"What? You think *you* could do it?" Sam pulled Diego to a halt.

Ethan stopped Miss Priss and urged the mare in a circle to face Sam. She tried not to be impressed at the easy movements he used, as if he'd been doing it for years instead of days. Ethan shrugged. "It can't be that hard."

"In that case, why don't you come out with Cole later and let him show you the ropes?" Sam snorted. Less than a week on a horse and Ethan thought he was a real working cowboy? Typical. "You'll think twice."

"Oh, yeah?" Ethan shifted in the saddle. "I think I could pick it up after one try."

"One section of fence, and you're an expert? I'd let Cole be the judge of that."

"Then let him." Ethan grinned. "What do you say?"

Sam tilted her head. "All right. Kate and I were planning on going to the Appleback street fair tomorrow night. I say if you don't—under Cole's supervision—fix any broken fence within two hours' time, then you have to sign up for the dunking booth."

"And if I make the deadline?"

Sam pursed her lips. "You won't."

"But if I do..." Ethan's eyes glimmered in challenge. "You have to enter."

Sam sidled Diego up close to Miss Priss and offered her hand to Ethan. "Deal."

They shook, and Sam smirked. She couldn't wait to see Ethan and his trademark polo floating in a pool of water.

Ethan winced as another barb bit into his glove. Cole, several feet down by the post, shot him a knowing look and Ethan tugged harder at the fencing despite his screaming biceps. He couldn't let Cole know he was struggling, or the cowboy wouldn't tell Sam that Ethan did the job correctly. The only thing worse than splashing into a small town's annual dunking booth would be the gloating look on Sam's face if he lost.

He pulled again. No matter who won, at least Ethan had a date to the fair. Sam never would have considered inviting him to come with her and Kate otherwise. Ethan wrinkled his brow. Invited, challenged—same difference, right? Regardless, Ethan now had tangible proof to show his father he was spending time with Sam doing fun things. Bottom line—if he was with her, Daniel wouldn't have a chance to move in. Never had appearances become so important.

And never had a work project become this complicated.

He shuddered at the thought of his father finding out Ethan's real plans to leave the company. He pushed aside the thought and concentrated on the physical ache in his muscles. He'd never worked so hard, but the thought of getting to spend tomorrow with Sam in a non-chore atmosphere made sweating over a prickly pile of fencing almost worth it.

Although, on second thought, it would be awfully hard to explain to his dad why he was out in a pasture in the middle of the afternoon, helping to repair a fence instead of working to destroy it as Jeffrey requested. The complications kept piling up. It'd be pretty simple to sabotage the fence, even under Cole's scrutiny. But Ethan refused to participate in his father's devious plans. He'd rather make excuses to his dad than hurt Sam any more than he was already going to have to.

"How does this work, exactly?" Ethan strained harder and his gloves slipped. The fencing snapped free and fell to the ground in a messy tangle of wire. He sucked in his breath. Now he'd done it. Once Sam heard about this, he'd lose for sure. He turned his gaze to Cole, who snickered.

"Guess this might be a good time to introduce you to a little thing I like to call a fence stretcher." Cole held up a long yellow tool and grinned.

Ethan's mouth opened. "You've got to be kidding me. How long were you going to let me pretend that I was being productive?"

"I reckon 'bout 'til you gave up."

"Great." Ethan ran his gloved hand over his face and groaned.

Cole began stringing the wire through the machine. "Don't worry, I won't tell Sam. I know about your little challenge."

Ethan's eyes narrowed. "Why would you help me?"

"Sam needs a dose of her own medicine now and then." Cole pushed his cowboy hat back with one hand. "Besides, it'd be pretty funny to see her in that dunking booth. She takes herself too seriously."

"So you're going to tell her I fixed the fence?" Ethan couldn't believe what he was hearing.

"Reckon there's no reason not to—because that's exactly what you're going to do." Cole's face drifted back into his usual scowl. "Now get over here, you're not getting out of this without some work."

Ethan scrambled to follow the cowboy's orders, his heart light for the first time in days. He couldn't wait to see the look on Sam's face when Cole gave her the progress report, or hear the inevitable scream when Sam realized what she'd agreed to. He checked his watch and winced. They'd be cutting it close.

He took the tool from Cole and got to work.

Sam almost swallowed her gum as she glimpsed Ethan and Cole riding toward the barn on Miss Priss and Salsa—laughing. She'd figured Cole would have torn Ethan to shreds after hours of fence repair—both physically and emotionally. But the smile Ethan wore as the twosome dismounted by the stable was brighter than the stars beginning to poke through the navy sky.

She hesitantly made her way toward them, automatically reaching out to take Miss Priss's reins from Ethan.

"I've got her." Ethan's hair, mussed, sweaty and without an ounce of leftover gel, flopped on his forehead and he shook it back with a grin. "A man's got to finish what he starts, right?" He nodded once at Cole before leading Miss Priss into the barn.

Sam turned toward Cole and fisted her hands on her hips. "Okay, what happened out there? You two left as Felix and Oscar from *The Odd Couple,* and came back all buddy-buddy."

Cole unbuckled the girth and tugged the saddle from his mount's back. "Ethan did it." He hefted the saddle onto the fence rail.

"Did what?" Sam reached out to balance the saddle while Cole removed the blanket from the horse.

"Repaired the fence."

Sam shook her head. "Impossible."

"He did the work. Why would I lie?" Cole draped the blanket over one arm and held out both hands for the saddle.

Sam dropped the leather seat over Cole's arm a little harder than necessary and he staggered backward under the sudden weight. "He knows nothing about fences. Or riding. Or horses." Her blood pulsed fiery hot in her veins. No way did Ethan stroll out to the pasture and easily repair a barbed-wire fence, even with Cole's help. Who did he think he was, The Lone Ranger?

"He's a fast learner." Cole turned toward the barn with a little shrug. "What can I say?"

Sam's eyes narrowed as Cole disappeared into the shadows of the stable. Beside her, Salsa nickered and Sam rubbed his hairy cheek. "Those two are up to something." Salsa tossed his neck as if in agreement.

Reality sounded like a clanging dinner bell and Sam sucked in her breath. If she kept to her word, she was now officially an entrant in the Appleback fair dunking booth. Her stomach flipped at the thought of that cold, dirty water. Cole must have somehow heard about the challenge and lied about Ethan's progress as a joke. That would explain Ethan's sudden aptitude for fence work.

Ethan strode back outside to the paddock and looped his arms over the top rail. "Did you hear the good news?" He grinned.

She tugged at Salsa's reins to lead the horse forward, but Ethan followed close beside her. "So? Did Cole tell you?"

Sam turned to go around him, but it was like backing a trailer into a narrow driveway—hard. She stopped walking. "He lied to me about your work, if that's what you mean."

Ethan's expression tightened. "Do you really think I'm that incompetent?"

"Maybe not at accounting or consulting or whatever it is you do for your millions." Sam sidestepped him again, and Salsa's hoof narrowly missed Sam's boot. "But at ranch life, yes."

"So all this work I've been doing the past several days—none of it matters to you?" Ethan's features hardened to stone.

Sam's mouth opened and closed. It did matter—that was the problem. Ethan was picking up the rhythm of the farm faster than Sam could have ever expected, and for some reason, it bothered her more than she wanted to admit. "Whatever." She started once again for the barn. No time to think about such things, not with Salsa needing to be untacked and Sam's midnight practice ride on Lucy to think about. There were bigger issues at stake, bigger than a street fair and bigger than Ethan's wounded feelings.

Bigger than her heart demanding an evaluation.

Ethan caught her arm. "Listen, Cole knew about our deal. He said he'd cover for me, because he wanted to play a joke on you. But I really did the work on the fence after he showed me how the fence stretcher operated. He isn't lying."

Salsa snorted over Sam's shoulder and she leaned against the horse's neck, enjoying the warmth against the cool evening air and the comfort of the familiar touch against her back. If people could be even half as understanding and sympathetic as horses, the world would be a better place.

"Do you believe me?" Ethan inched closer, his breath teasing her hair.

She didn't want to say yes. It'd be much easier to believe Ethan was just a rich New Yorker who couldn't put his boots on the right feet; much easier to believe the guys just wanted to pull a prank on her over the dunking booth. But the look in Ethan's gaze proved it was more than that. And if she looked closer—*way* more.

Sam abruptly straightened. "I believe you." She had to tell the truth. But she didn't have to tell how her stomach did a boot-scootin' line dance at Ethan's close proximity.

"Good." Ethan eased slightly away, not breaking eye contact. "So, tomorrow night? You, me and the fair?"

"And Kate," Sam reminded. Her heart stammered and she blamed it on too much caffeine. Definitely not because of those heartfelt brown orbs trying to burrow into her defenses.

"Right. Well, you better bring your pitchin' arm."

Sam paused. "Me? What do you mean?"

"You never let me finish. I did the work—but it took longer than two hours." His lips twisted to the side in mock disgust. "Two hours and twenty minutes. I'm pretty sure Cole won't ever let me forget that."

Sam's eyes widened. "So you're going to sit in the tank?" Him. Not her. She let out a slow breath of relief. Talk about a close one.

"That was the deal, wasn't it? And here you thought I wasn't honest." Ethan shoved away from the fence with a smile.

As hard as Sam tried to pull up her previous frustration, all she could do was smile back.

Chapter Twelve

"Step right up, folks. That's right, step right up here and I'll show you a cowboy in a box." The man in a large hat and striped pants on stilts, who Sam knew was really Bobby Gillum from the Grill My Grits Diner on Main Street, teetered near the tank where Ethan perched on a wooden collapsible seat wearing an oversize rubber cowboy hat. "That's right, a cowboy destined to get soaked."

Sam laughed at Bobby's circus-announcer impersonation—he really should have practiced his bit a little more—and waved at Ethan, who adjusted his position on the wobbling board. She couldn't help but grin. He waved back, his expression dubious as he glanced down at the water lapping at his dangling feet.

Kate and Daniel—he just *had* to tag along uninvited when he'd heard of their plans—had left a few minutes ago to snag some cotton candy for the three of them. Sam was waiting until they got back to take her turn. So far, Ethan had been fortunate. There'd been nothing but a crowd of overeager Little Leaguers with bad aim and a few gnarled old-timers who'd attempted to soak him. He remained dry—for now.

Kate appeared at Sam's side, cotton candy in hand. "What'd I miss?"

"Nothing yet." Sam turned to Bobby. "I'll take a shot." The gathering afternoon crowd parted and murmured their approval as she made her way to the front. She handed Bobby three red tickets and plucked a softball from the bucket.

"Give the lady some room, folks," Bobby boomed, stumbling toward the crowd and waving his hands to clear the area. "This one looks like a winner!"

Ethan crossed his arms over his chest and waited, his dimples making a defiant appearance on his tanned cheeks. He shook his head. "She needs all the room she can get—and a little luck!"

"Sounds like fighting words," Bobby teased. "Come on, Miss. Let's see what you got."

Sam wound her arm a few times to loosen the muscles and drove the ball toward the target. It bounced harmlessly off the plastic net. The crowd booed.

"Wow, look at those muscles." A college-aged girl standing near Sam nudged her friend in the side, her eyes riveted on Ethan.

A prick of jealousy snagged Sam's stomach. She shouldn't care what a bouncy little blonde teen thought of him. But Ethan didn't even seem to notice the girls, as he kept his eyes trained on Sam—and winked.

Her heart stuttered, and she quickly prepared her next shot. *Focus, focus.*

Bam. The ball slammed against the target and Ethan splashed into the murky water. Sam gasped and then threw her arms in the air in victory. "Yes!"

He resurfaced with a gasp for air and sloshed his hair back from his eyes. The crowd roared with laughter and Sam offered a sheepish shrug. Kate grinned around her cone of cotton candy and Daniel shook his head with a smile, as if he knew Sam was going to hear about it from Ethan later and he couldn't wait to watch.

With all the dignity Ethan could muster—which wasn't much, as most of it still floated with the dirty water in the tank—he struggled back onto the seat and waved good-naturedly to the taunting crowd.

Then his eyes met Sam's and she felt as if she was the one drowning.

Ethan changed clothes inside the public fairground restrooms and joined Kate, Daniel and Sam back outside. He shook his head at Daniel's offer of cotton candy.

"Good thing you don't have my red hair and matching temper." Kate grinned, bits of pink sugar stuck to her cheeks. "Or Sam would be in trouble right now."

Ethan shoved his hands in his jeans pockets, and offered Sam an easy smile. "Hey, I agreed to the dare, fair and square. I had to pay my dues—even if she was the only one to soak me during my entire shift." He nudged her with his elbow.

"What can I say? I have good aim." Sam nudged back, her light brown hair pulled up in a high ponytail. Already loose tendrils escaped around her face. She looked prettier than any city girl he'd ever seen in New York—and with apparently little effort. Ethan's breath hitched and he tried to cover the hiccup sound with a cough.

"What, no fight? That's no fun." Daniel tossed his cone into a nearby trash can. "I was all fired up for a blow-out between you two." He laughed.

"You want fun? Let's hit the Gravy Train. It's the fastest roller coaster this side of the Mississippi." Kate threw away her nearly empty cone of sugar and wiped her hands on her jeans. Pink tufts stuck to the back pockets but she didn't seem to care as Daniel offered her his arm.

"M'lady." He winked over his shoulder at Ethan as they led the way toward the rides.

Ethan fell into step beside Sam. "Looks like those two are hitting it off."

Sam's eyes narrowed as she studied the couple in front of them. Daniel ducked his head low and Kate laughed at his murmured comment. "Seems that way."

"Do I detect a bit of regret in those words?"

"I don't know about regret, but I don't see anything positive forming out of a friendship with those two."

"Why not?" Ethan slowed his pace to match Sam's, ambling beside her as the sun set behind the Ferris wheel in the near distance, scattering bits of pink and purple and orange across the sky. *He* knew why Daniel shouldn't get close to Kate, or any other self-respecting woman, but Sam couldn't know that about him this soon.

"They're too different." Sam gestured toward the couple now several steps ahead. "City boy, country girl. What does Daniel know about horses and ranch life? And what does Kate know about designer labels or foreign cities? They have nothing in common."

"Sort of like us." The blow of Sam's words hit a soft spot in Ethan's heart that had long been forming. He'd hoped it would have calloused by now, but no such luck. The words pricked sharper than Cupid's bow but without the mushy, pain-relieving side effects. He averted his gaze so Sam wouldn't see the disappointment he knew welled in his eyes.

Sam stopped. "I didn't mean it like—I just..." She blew out her breath and shoved her hands in her pockets. "Forget I said anything." She began walking again, faster than before.

"It's true, though, isn't it?" Not wanting to continue the conversation but somehow unable to stop himself, Ethan hurried after her. "Just say it."

"Say what, Ethan?" Sam wheeled in front of him, and he nearly ran into her. "Say that we're from two different worlds and have nothing in common, either? Why does it matter?" Her gaze searched his, undefined emotion deepening the blue to cobalt.

Ethan looked over her shoulder at the Ferris wheel on the horizon. A dozen thoughts vied for release in his mouth, but he swallowed them as a new idea struck. "Take a ride with me."

"What?" Sam's eyebrows shot up with surprise.

"Take a ride with me." He grabbed her hand, pulled her toward the ticket booth and handed the cashier a ten dollar bill. "Come on." He pocketed the string of red squares and plowed through the throng of people.

"Where are we going?" Sam tugged at his grip, but Ethan held her hand tighter as he maneuvered a path through the thickening evening crowd. He couldn't let go now, or the crowd would swallow her whole.

"Here." Breathless, Ethan drew Sam to a stop at the line for the Ferris wheel. She tilted her head back, peering up at the brightly lit cars making their way around the giant circle.

"The Ferris wheel?" Her brow furrowed with doubt.

"It's a classic."

"What about the Gravy Train?"

"I get enough of the fast life in New York." He paused until Sam's gaze locked with his. "I'm ready to slow things down."

Their car stopped two from the top of the wheel, and Sam didn't know if it was the height or Ethan's nearness that put her nerves on red alert. What had he meant by saying he wanted to slow things down? Was he talking about life in general, or about her? She drew a deep breath, her mind racing almost as fast as the Gravy Train she could see across the park, a whirl of lights and music as the cars raced around a shiny red track. Apparently Kate and Daniel hadn't missed them after Ethan's mad dash to the ticket booth, as Sam's cell phone hadn't vibrated once in her pocket.

"It's nice up here, isn't it?" The wind brushed strands of dark hair out of Ethan's eyes. He must have skipped the gel after the dunk tank, and Sam was surprised at his hair's length. It seemed longer than a typical cut for a business professional, and she couldn't imagine Ethan doing anything outside the book. But maybe there was more depth to him than she'd originally thought.

The idea struck Sam with a shameful dose of clarity. Hadn't Ethan already proven that enough times with his hard work around the ranch? No wonder he'd been so offended when she questioned his capability on repairing fences. An apology rose in her throat and stuck on her lips. "Ethan, I—"

He turned to her, their faces only inches apart. Her stomach tingled and Sam froze. Ethan's hand found hers and he ran his fingers lightly over her knuckles. "Yes?"

She tried to breathe, but couldn't remember her name, much less what she'd been about to say. "I—" She swallowed. His gaze bore into hers, drawing her in as he leaned closer. Sam followed the magnetic pull, the lights of the Ferris wheel a romantic glow in her peripheral vision. "I—" Her hands shook, and she clenched her free one in her lap. Desperate to speak but scared of the words that might roll off her tongue.

Ethan's cell rang, jangling Sam out of her thoughts and jarring her back to reality with a resounding crash. She jerked away from Ethan, causing their little car to sway, and he grabbed for his phone. "Hello?"

Daniel's voice rose through the phone above the crowd and the music. He shouted something she couldn't decipher as Sam's stomach churned. And this time there was no food to blame.

"We're at the Ferris wheel. We'll meet you by the corn dog stand in about fifteen minutes." Ethan dropped his cell into his shirt pocket, and released a long breath. "Sorry about that."

Sam nodded and forced a smile, but her thoughts were galloping much further ahead. She'd almost kissed Ethan. What was she thinking? It'd be like pairing a goat with a Thoroughbred—impossible. They were on completely different levels of life in status, mindset, goals. Some things just weren't meant to be—even if under the glow of the stars it seemed as if, for a moment, they could.

Sam turned to look out her side of the car as the wheel gently lowered them back to earth.

Chapter Thirteen

The lights and music of the fairgrounds seemed to lose their magic as Ethan and Sam joined Kate and Daniel at the corn dog stand. Earlier Ethan had been contemplating buying a dog, but now his stomach twisted into knots and made food undesirable.

He'd almost kissed Sam. What kind of idiot was he? If he wasn't careful, he'd easily cross the professional line with Sam that he'd been so concerned about Daniel crossing, and then Ethan wouldn't be any better than his womanizing cousin.

Sam joined Kate in line ahead of Ethan, tucking loose strands of hair behind her ears as she peered up at the neon menu. Was she really hungry, or was it all an act? Maybe she hadn't been affected by the near kiss after all. Maybe she hadn't even realized his intentions and Ethan was worrying for nothing.

And maybe all of this country air was getting to him. Ethan groaned. He was losing his mind to a cowgirl with wildflower blue eyes and a quick wit he had yet to find in the usual New York crowd—and rapidly losing his heart to a woman who'd never look twice at him. For once, his money and status wasn't enough, which just made him respect Sam even more. She looked deeper than his wallet, and it figured the one woman who had the maturity and grace to do so was the same one who needed a *real* man in her life—a cattle driver, not a paper pusher. He massaged his temples with his fingers.

"What's wrong? If you don't want a corn dog, we can grab a meat pie instead." Daniel gestured over his shoulder to the row of food booths lining the road.

"It's not the food."

"Ah." A knowing spark lit Daniel's eyes. "I didn't interrupt anything on the Ferris wheel, did I?" He nudged Ethan in the ribs.

"No! I mean, not really. Lower your voice." Ethan whispered, hoping Daniel would follow his cue. "This whole situation is getting sticky, that's all."

"What's sticky?" Kate's red head popped up from giving her order at the window and she stepped out of line with her change.

Ethan swallowed. "Um, the cotton candy."

Kate grinned and pocketed her change as Sam moved to join them, holding a large cup of lemonade.

"How was the roller coaster?" Sam took a sip from the straw.

Ethan frowned. Was she avoiding his eyes? Or was he being paranoid? They really should talk soon, or else working together the rest of his stay at the ranch was going to be more than a little awkward.

He was leaving in two weeks, maybe sooner if his father had his way. His family would eventually get what they needed and go back to New York, slimy contract in hand. To Sam, Ethan would be nothing more than a harsh memory—the man who stole the family farm out from under her and turned a pile of precious earth and memories into concrete and clearance racks. His stomach churned again. Definitely no room for a corn dog with this much guilt taking up space.

"The roller coaster was fun." Kate grinned around her mustard-covered corn dog at Ethan. "Even if your cousin did scream like a girl."

"I did not." Daniel lifted his chin and brushed at the shoulder of his shirt with a fake air of dignity. "I just yelled. Loudly and repeatedly."

"We told you it was fast." Sam laughed.

"How was the Ferris wheel?" Daniel's teasing gaze pierced Ethan until the spark left and all that remained in Daniel's eyes was pointed animosity.

"Great, like I said earlier." Ethan stared back just as intensely, hoping Daniel would detour from the verbal path he was taking. That conversation would lead nowhere productive, and could only further drive a wedge between Ethan and Sam. Or is that what Daniel wanted?

They locked gazes for several moments until Daniel finally blinked, looked away and grinned down at Sam. "Next time you should ride with me." He met Ethan's eyes again in a brief challenge.

Ethan glimpsed Kate's frown. He drew a deep breath. Great. He'd somehow offended Daniel with his back-off vibe regarding Sam, and now his cousin was in it for keeps. Ethan could only hope Sam wouldn't fall for such a tacky, obvious play.

But she seemed oblivious to the tension—and to the fact that Kate's eyes were narrowing to tiny slits. Jealousy? Ethan wished he could bang his head against the giant sign shaped like a corn dog. The children's game *Which of these does not belong?* popped into his mind, and Ethan grimaced. The answer was depressingly easy—none of them. He didn't belong with Sam, Kate didn't belong with Daniel, Sam didn't belong with Daniel or vice versa…Ethan's headache roared and he shut his eyes against the throbbing. So much for a fun night on the town. He'd rather be scooping manure.

"Hey, look, Sam." Kate pointed across the grounds to a tent set up by the ice cream stand. "A mechanical bull. That'd be extra practice for you."

Ethan's eyes widened. Daniel didn't know about Sam's plan to bull-ride. How could Kate have slipped up like that with her best friend's secret? He glanced at Sam. Panic shadowed her expression.

Kate glanced between Sam and Ethan. "What? I told Daniel about Sam's plans when we were in line for the roller coaster. He thought it was great. Really bold."

Sam's face paled. Ethan bit down on his lower lip. *Not good, not good…*

"Hey, it's cool with me." Daniel shrugged, but his gaze held an ulterior motive. "I won't tell anyone."

Kate's brow furrowed in concern. "I figured if Ethan knew, there was no reason for his cousin not to. I'm sorry, Sam."

Sam drew a deep breath and the paper cup in her hand wobbled slightly. "It's okay. No big deal."

But Ethan could tell it wasn't okay. Apparently Sam could see for herself that telling Ethan a secret and confiding the same to Daniel was the difference between trusting a sheep and a wolf. If Daniel passed the info to Jeffrey, he would have not only one-upped Ethan again, he would sabotage the ranch even further—exactly as Jeffrey hoped.

Ethan felt Sam's gaze on him and offered her a smile he hoped didn't look as forced as it felt. "How about that ride, cowgirl?"

"On a mechanical bull?" Sam laughed, but the worry in her eyes hadn't completely faded. "No, thanks. Lucy could take on that piece of metal in a heartbeat. What's the point?"

"You think riding Lucy is harder than staying on that thing?" Kate pointed to the machine, which whirled in a sharp, tight circle before dumping a thin cowboy on the padded mats below. He stood up and slapped his hat against his leg in disgust before ambling out the open-sided tent.

Sam's lips twisted. "Maybe not."

"Don't tell me you're scared." Daniel's arm landed around Sam's shoulders and she stiffened almost as fast as Ethan did. He fought the impulse to rake his cousin's arm away. Starting a fight would only lead to disaster, and Ethan could only guess whose side his father would take once he heard.

Sam eased away from Daniel's casual touch without prompting and Ethan let out his breath in relief. "You should go for it, Sam. In fact, I'll do it, too."

Daniel's brow rose and he lowered his rejected arm to his side. "In that case, count me in."

"You? On a bull?" Ethan snorted.

Daniel glared. "It's not like it's real. Besides, if you can do it, I can do it."

They squared off and Ethan worked to control the harsh words threatening to fly from his lips. What was Daniel's problem? Why had he suddenly decided to go after Sam? And why bother flirting with Kate if Sam was his goal all along? His cousin had just said at the lodge that he would back off for Ethan's sake. Had Jeffrey anted up the pressure since then?

"You're all crazy. I'll be just fine watching from the sidelines." Kate smirked. "Besides, Sam will beat you both."

"We'll see about that." Daniel winked at Sam again and she quickly looked the other way.

"After you." Ethan gestured for Sam to go ahead of him,

The Reader Service - Here's how it works:

Accepting your 2 free books and 2 free mystery gifts places you under no obligation to buy anything. You may keep the books and gifts and return the shippin statement marked "cancel." If you do not cancel, about a month later we'll send you 6 additional books and bill you just $4.24 each for the regular-print editio or $4.74 each for the larger-print edition in the U.S. or $4.74 each for the regular-print edition or $5.24 each for the larger-print edition in Canada. That's savings of at least 20% off the cover price. It's quite a bargain! Shipping and handling is just 50¢ per book.* You may cancel at any time, but if you choose t continue, every month we'll send you 6 more books, which you may either purchase at the discount price or return to us and cancel your subscription.

*Terms and prices subject to change without notice. Prices do not include applicable taxes. Sales tax applicable in N.Y. Canadian residents will be charge applicable provincial taxes and GST. Offer not valid in Quebec. All orders subject to approval. Books received may not be as shown. Credit or debit balances i a customer's account(s) may be offset by any other outstanding balance owed by or to the customer. Please allow 4 to 6 weeks for delivery. Offer availabl while quantities last.

If offer card is missing, write to The Reader Service, P.O. Box 1867, Buffalo, NY 14240-1867
or visit: www.ReaderService.com

BUSINESS REPLY MAIL

FIRST-CLASS MAIL PERMIT NO. 717 BUFFALO, NY

POSTAGE WILL BE PAID BY ADDRESSEE

THE READER SERVICE
PO BOX 1867
BUFFALO NY 14240-9952

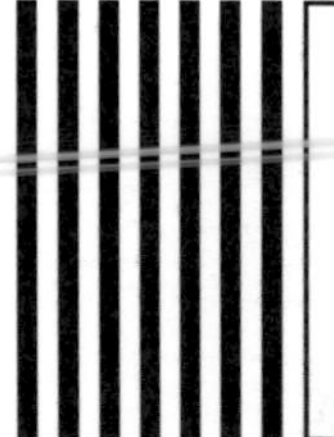

then purposefully shouldered past Daniel to fall into step behind her. He might be about to take on his first bull, but he had a feeling the battle with Daniel was just beginning.

Back on a bull again. This time, it was a mixture of faux hair and steel instead of hide and sweat. Still, the nerves in her stomach reminded Sam of what was at stake—not only her dignity, but her ranch. If she couldn't stay on a fake bull, how could she manage a real one in two weeks? No bull, no cash, no stallion, no breeding farm. The equation was painfully simple.

Although according to Daniel and Ethan and the way they kept acting like Neanderthals, one would think the only issue currently at stake was Sam's heart. Any minute now she half expected one of them to grab her ponytail and drag her away as a prize. What was with their sudden testosterone battle? Daniel had ridden the mechanical bull first and fallen after a measly three seconds. One good twist of the machine and he'd slipped onto the mats with a scowl. Ethan had gone next and done better by maybe a full second, but from the look in his eyes, any time longer than Daniel's was enough.

Sam had to ride well—not just for the sake of proving to herself she could actually have a shot at that rodeo prize money, but for the sake of holding her own against two pompous city slickers.

Even if one of them did smell like spicy cologne and had eyes that made Sam's stomach flip like a flapjack on a griddle.

"You ready, little lady?" The older man in jean overalls and a T-shirt working the switchboard control shifted in his metal folding chair, which squeaked in protest under his weight. Sam grasped the padded handle on the bull, took a deep breath and nodded.

With a squeaky groan, the machine sprung to life and whipped Sam to the left. Then to the right. She hung on and fought the urge to grab the horn with her free hand. At least this way if she fell, it'd be on foam and not hard-packed dirt.

But this bull was much feistier than Lucy. Sam's head jerked to the side and she struggled to maintain her balance. The slick rubber wasn't as easy for her legs to grip as they did on the real steer. She wobbled dangerously to one side. *Hang on, hang on.* She couldn't let Ethan or Daniel win.

She glimpsed the figures of her friends—did she consider Ethan and Daniel friends now?—standing to one side of the tent, clapping and yelling. Kate's unmistakable two-fingered whistle split the air and Sam gripped harder with her thighs. "Seven seconds," Kate screamed in encouragement.

The world flew by in a blur of red tent stripes and blue gym mats. Her fingers suddenly slipped and Sam sprawled on the ground in a heap.

"You did it!" Ethan rushed Sam before she could stand and hauled her to her feet. "Nine seconds!" His arms wrapped around her in a tight hug and Sam inhaled his masculine scent. Her arms automatically curled around his neck. Over his shoulder, Kate's eyes widened and her lips parted in shock.

Sam backed slowly away from Ethan's embrace, heat flushing her face. She couldn't believe she'd thrown herself into his arms like that. She really couldn't believe the envy that sprang onto Daniel's face as if he'd suddenly chomped into a lemon.

But most of all, she couldn't believe the impulse to kiss Ethan was back, even stronger than it had been on the Ferris wheel.

Chapter Fourteen

The next morning, Sam practically tip-toed into the barn. Maybe Ethan wasn't up yet. Maybe he'd overslept and wouldn't be helping with the morning chores today.

Maybe he'd forgotten about the way she'd thrown herself into his embrace and hugged him after staying on the bull for the required eight seconds.

Sam's cheeks heated. What a ridiculous victory in the first place. It wasn't like she'd ridden a real bull or accomplished anything other than proving she could linger on a piece of moving steel longer than two greenhorn men. What was worth celebrating about that? It didn't change her circumstances, didn't change the fact that her family's farm was still broke and in danger of moving further into the red every day. No, it didn't change anything—even if Ethan's hug had felt like a tiny piece of home.

Still, the question remained—why was Ethan so excited for her about the riding success when just two days ago he'd been trying to talk Sam out of entering the rodeo? Something was up with Ethan, something strange about his family—and it had nothing to do with Vickie's fashion choices, Jeffrey's absence from activities, or Daniel's flirtation attempts. Maybe Sam was just imagining things because she wanted them to leave so badly.

She drew a tight breath. Was that a past tense "wanted," or present tense? Ethan *had* been a big help to her with the morning chores, leaving Cole available to handle bigger tasks he'd never had the time for. Not to mention having someone to talk to other than the horses made the menial duties more enjoyable. Somehow, Ethan's being at the ranch was becoming less of a hassle and more of a…blessing?

The morning was turning into a brain teaser.

Sam reached for the pitchfork in the barn's supply closet. The wooden stick felt heavy in her hands, and soreness radiated from her shoulder. All those late nights of practicing on Lucy were starting to show, not to mention the core-strengthening exercises Cole was making her do, and her muscles were suffering from it. Would it even matter? Would it be enough?

She shut the door and headed to the first stall. She hated these moments of self-doubt, hated bearing the burden of such pressure. Other women her age at the church were married, some even had kids or were thinking about children. The few single ones left in her class—the last time Sam went, anyway—were satisfied in their careers or pursuing graduate degrees.

Would Sam ever feel free to live her own life?

A figure, shadowed against the morning light streaming into the barn, appeared in the doorway of the stables and Sam hesitated before walking into Wildfire's stall. Ethan. She lifted her hand in a quick wave and slipped under Wildfire's neck to secure his halter. Her fingers fumbled with the familiar buckles and her heart raced. *Calm down. It's just Ethan—the same guy who got on your last nerve just a few days ago.* Technically, nothing had changed. But try telling that to her shaky hands.

Sam jumped as Ethan popped his head over the half stall door. "Good morning."

"Mornin'." She avoided his eyes, hoping the blush had faded from her cheeks by now. She let her hair block his view of her face as she finally managed to buckle the halter on Wildfire.

"Did you practice with Lucy last night? I crashed after we got home from the fair." Ethan's voice, rich and invigorating like morning coffee, warmed Sam's insides.

"No, I took the night off." She spoke into her curtain of brown hair as she clipped the lead rope onto the halter. "One crazy ride was enough for the evening."

"I bet so. Daniel's still asleep. He said he was sore from his ride." Ethan snorted. "Attempted ride, anyway." He opened the stall door for Sam to lead Wildfire out, without her having to ask.

Sam guided the horse into the aisle, unable to resist taking a poke at Ethan's bubble of pride. "You didn't stay on much longer than your cousin."

Ethan shrugged. "Hey, a second longer is a second longer." He grinned.

Sam quickly looked away before her empty stomach could start fluttering again. "Would you mind cleaning Wildfire's stall? I'm going to put him in the pasture and then come back for Piper."

"Sure." Ethan grabbed the pitchfork without complaint and disappeared inside the pen.

Sam slowly led Wildfire toward the stable doors. Maybe Ethan hadn't noticed how his presence affected her, made her voice falter and heated her stomach like the dead of summer. If she was lucky, she could keep up the indifferent act until these feelings of attraction went away. At best, she and Ethan could be friends until his vacation ended. Anything more was asking for trouble. They were from completely different worlds, and Ethan was leaving hers in two weeks.

The only thing harder than trying to save her family farm would be trying to save it with a broken heart.

Ethan dumped the last wheelbarrow load of manure into the compost pile and headed back into the barn. The last stall was done. Sam had been absent for a good thirty minutes now, but he didn't mind doing the hard work alone. At least that way he didn't have to think about kissing her—or worse, not kissing her—again.

Ethan steered the wheelbarrow into the supply closet. He wasn't sure what brought on that spontaneous hug last night after her ride. Maybe he'd just gotten caught up in the competition and excitement of seeing Sam succeed, watching her achieve a goal he knew was so important to her. The question was, when had Sam's personal goals become so important to *him?*

He shook his head as he shut the closet door. Regardless, she'd felt really good in his arms—like she belonged. That was a dangerous fact to analyze, but right or wrong, it was there, unwilling to be ignored.

He looked up as Sam trudged toward him from the opposite end of the aisle, her expression pinched.

"Would you mind going with me into town? I need to pick up the feed order, and Cole's stuck giving private riding lessons to a guest." Sam stopped several feet away and shoved her fingertips in her jeans pockets. "I might need help loading the bags into the back of the truck. Sometimes if the store is too busy, the workers don't have time."

"No problem. I just finished mucking out the stalls." Ethan gestured toward the rows of pens.

"All of them?" Sam's brows shot upward. "In half an hour? I'm impressed."

Finally. Ethan smiled, hoping his relief didn't show on his face. Who knew hauling manure would be the way into a girl's heart?

Sam's expression softened and she pulled a ring of keys from her pocket. "Ready to go?"

He nodded. "I'm ready if you are." Ethan followed Sam out of the stable and to the parking lot by the main house. *Ready or not.*

Miles of interstate uncurled before them through the front window of the truck like a winding yellow ribbon. Sam kept her booted foot steady on the gas pedal. The trip into town seemed much longer than it had last night heading to the fair, the cab now filled with silence and the heady aroma of Ethan's freshly applied cologne instead of Kate and Daniel's jokes and laughter. Sam preferred the quietness, though awkward at times, to the constant noise and teasing of the evening before. From the contented expression Ethan wore as he gazed out the window, it appeared he felt the same.

Maybe they weren't so entirely different after all.

Sam clicked on her blinker as she eased around a slow-moving sedan in the fast lane. "You'd think they'd stick to the right lane if they insist on going ten under the speed limit."

Ethan laughed. "I'm usually the one going at least ten over."

Sam sent him a sidelong glance.

"Okay, okay, more like fifteen or twenty."

"I thought so, after you way you peeled into the parking

lot of the ranch your first day here like you were gearing up for the Indy."

Ethan grinned. "So you were watching me?"

Sam swallowed hard. Busted. She stared at the road, racking her brain for a way to retract the blunder without lying. "How could I not after that dramatic arrival?"

"Now you sound like my dad." The teasing light faded from Ethan's expression.

Sam glanced at the road, then back at Ethan's slight frown. "What do you mean?"

"He thinks all I'm good for is sports cars. Just because they're interesting to me doesn't mean it's all I can do."

An oppressing silence filled the cab, broken only by the loud gush of the air conditioner. Sam reached over and clicked the knob to a lower setting. The whooshing immediately quieted. "I'm sure your dad doesn't actually think that."

"Trust me, he does." Ethan rubbed his hand over his forehead. "But let's not ruin a nice afternoon by talking about my father, okay?"

Sam's hands tightened on the steering wheel. "At least you have a father to argue with."

Ethan's expression contorted and he touched Sam's shoulder. The contact sparked up her arm and her hands shook on the wheel, for a variety of reasons she refused to acknowledge. "I'm sorry." His voice, void of the bitterness it held moments before, lowered with regret. "I wasn't thinking."

Sam inhaled, shrugging her shoulders up so Ethan's hand fell back to his side. "Don't worry about it. But next time you feel like complaining about your father, remember not everyone has that luxury." She exited the highway and turned left toward the feed store.

"Point taken." Ethan ran his hand over his hair, then stared forward, his profile a tight, indiscernible mask. "But you need to remember not everyone's family life is as happy as yours apparently used to be."

Ethan wasn't used to being spoken to so bluntly by a woman—and judging by the shocked expression on Sam's face, she wasn't used to hearing an equal retort, either. But she'd handled it well, pressing her lips together into a tight line as she jammed the truck into Park in front of an aluminum-sided building. Multiple trucks and trailers crowded the small dirt lot, and several people in cowboy hats milled around the front porch.

"They look busy, so I guess you'll have to help me load after all. Ready to work?" Sam's smile, forcibly bright, looked pasted on her face. He had offended her, but she wasn't about to admit it.

Letting her off the hook, Ethan nodded. "Always." He slid out of the cab, ignoring her snort of derision. Sam slammed the door on her side and marched toward the building. Ethan followed her up the rickety front steps, his head barely clearing a crooked, low-hanging sign marked Smithson's Co-Op. A cowboy standing to one side of the porch nodded once as they passed, then spit tobacco into a plastic cup. Ethan inched closer behind Sam to shield her from the cowboy's appreciative backward glance.

Oblivious to her charm, Sam entered the fluorescence-lit shop with a wave to the denim-clad man behind the counter. "Mornin', Harry. I need the usual."

"Howdy there, Sam." Harry's voice boomed across the store as he tossed a pen on the mass of papers covering the counter. He shuffled his bulk to the ancient cash register, which, upon closer inspection, Ethan decided could have easily been the very first register ever made. How did that thing even work? Harry punched in some keys and Sam handed over her company credit card.

"Who's your friend there?" Harry peered at Ethan from beneath bushy eyebrows. Ethan bristled under the inspection. At least he was wearing his tennis shoes today and not loafers—though he had the instinctive feeling Harry could probably spot a city slicker a mile away. Why he felt the need to measure up to this man, Ethan had no idea, but he straightened his shoulders and gave his best smile.

"This is Ethan. His family is visiting our ranch and he offered to give me a hand loading the feed."

"Mighty nice of him." Harry looked suspiciously at Ethan as he zipped the credit card through a separate black machine.

Ethan pretended to study the gum selection at the counter. Was one expected to respond to an indirect, third-person reference? Sam was watching him, so he supposed so. He uttered a quick, "Thanks."

"Good thing, Billy out there is filling a big order for another ranch, and Tom called in sick today." Harry swiped the card a second time with a little frown. "I'm shorthanded as usual."

"No problem, Ethan and I can handle it." Sam smiled, but it faded as Harry zipped the card a third time. "Is there a problem?"

Harry leaned over the counter, his gravelly voice lowering to a whisper that could still be heard across the store. "Your card's been declined."

"What? I just paid— Oh, wait." Sam pulled in her lips and briefly closed her eyes. "Okay. That's fine. Can you bill us instead?"

Harry hesitated, and Sam's gaze turned pleading. "I'd like to, Sam, really I would, but your mother was late on her last bill and I can't afford—"

"Here, borrow mine." Ethan slipped a Visa card from his wallet and slid it to Harry. He elbowed Sam, trying to lighten the mood. "I know you're good for it."

Sam's face flushed scarlet but she didn't object, which spoke pretty highly of her desperation to get the horse feed. She shifted awkwardly beside him as Harry ran the card and handed the paper slip to Ethan to sign. He jotted his signature, glad he'd had the frame of mind to use his personal card instead of the company one, so at least his father wouldn't find out about the impromptu purchase. Jeffrey might be able to eventually understand how Ethan refused to sabotage the ranch, but he'd never understand him helping Sam financially. Ethan refused to let the horses go hungry at the cost of his company's gain.

The amount on the slip jumped out at Ethan as he handed Harry the signed copy. The horse feed wasn't that expensive. How bad off were the Jensons really? He tucked his copy in his jeans pocket before Sam could catch the surprised look on his face.

"You know where it all is, Sam. Help yourself." Harry gestured to the side door where Ethan could glimpse a loading platform and wheeled carts.

She smiled the same forced grin from before at Harry, lifted her hand in a slight wave and led Ethan to the loading dock.

Outside, Ethan gently caught her arm, turning her around. "Are you okay?"

"Fine." She averted her eyes. "You shouldn't have done that."

Ethan frowned. "Most people would just say thank you." He stepped aside to make room for another cowboy exiting the building and crossed his arms over his chest. Was she so prideful she couldn't accept a little help? A second look at her face proved it wasn't so much pride as it was embarrassment. His defensive guard lowered.

Sam drew in a tight breath. "You're right. Thank you."

"I'm not begging for compliments, Sam." Ethan fought the urge to pull her into his arms and hug away the wounded expression on her face. "Maybe the declined card was a mistake. It happens, you know?"

She turned away, out of his reach. "It wasn't a mistake. Trust me."

"Is your family going to be okay? I know you're riding to win money for the breeding business again, but I'm talking about basics. Food. Bills. Mortgage."

Sam kept walking, snagging one of the discarded metal dollies from beside the building and wheeling it toward the stacked bags of feed. "After your family pays us, we'll be fine."

Ethan froze on the concrete dock, her words hammering his heart like a construction worker on overtime. Sam was counting on their guest payment to cover their upcoming bills and keep the ranch going, all while Ethan's family was intending to buy the property out from under them. Angie Jenson might realize why they were there—or partly, anyway—but Sam didn't have a clue. He'd never even told her his real occupation.

Ethan's palms sweated and he clenched his fists. Sam might think he was some arrogant city slicker or a naive tourist, but he was worse, much worse.

Chapter Fifteen

"Declined?" Kate's eyes widened until her eyebrows practically disappeared into her red hair. She shook her head in sympathy as she readjusted her cross-legged position on the couch. "Sam, I had no idea things were that bad."

"I checked into it when we got home earlier today." Sam closed her eyes, temporarily blocking out the yellow, cheery atmosphere of Kate's cozy renovated farmhouse. If the room was to match Sam's current mood, it'd have to be painted charcoal-gray—with angry red slashes on the walls. "Apparently our business card was maxed out and we're two payments late on top of that. How could my mom not tell me?"

"Maybe she doesn't know." Kate's lips twisted as if even she knew the theory was too far-fetched to be truth.

"My mom has always handled our finances, even when Dad was alive. There's no way she'd forget to make payments. Obviously we can't afford them, and she kept it from me."

"Are you going to confront her about it?"

Sam leaned her head against the soft brown couch, exhaustion pinning her body against the leather. "No. I don't want her to be even more stressed than she already is. Plus she'll just try to bring up selling the ranch again."

"She probably didn't mean to keep it from you, but just didn't catch you before you went to the Co-op."

"Well, I don't know how she thinks we're going to pay the next month's feed supply at this point. Harry didn't seem very open to the idea of billing us." Sam pressed her fingers against her temples. "We're ruining our good name and reputation."

"I seriously doubt that. Everyone in Appleback loved your dad, and your family. Harry just has to watch out for his own company. He knows you'd never stiff him on purpose." Kate tossed a blue striped pillow at Sam. "Cheer up. Tell me about Ethan and Daniel." She grinned.

"What about them?" Sam hugged the little pillow to her chest. "Other than I made a fool of myself in front of Ethan—again. I have to find a way to pay him back for the feed supply. No way am I taking charity from him or anyone else."

"I don't blame you. Paying him back is the right thing to do, even if they can obviously afford that and more."

"No kidding." Sam sighed. "I just don't know why I keep goofing up in front of him. It's supposed to be the other way around. He'd never spent time on a farm, yet he's turning into a regular ranch hand. Go figure." She couldn't even be proud of his improvements because, somehow, buried under all the designer labels and hair gel, Ethan possessed a natural talent for all things ranching. If he ever wanted to start his own farm one day, then he'd have no trouble—with a little help, of course. Every ranch owner needed their own Cole.

"Ethan's a fast learner, huh? What about Daniel?" Kate's eyes lowered and she picked at a loose string on the arm of the couch. "I really am sorry I blurted your secret out like that at the fair. I thought if Ethan knew about the rodeo plans, then Daniel did."

Sam shrugged. "As long as my mom doesn't find out until after the competition, it doesn't matter."

"So you're really going to do it?" Kate kept her eyes averted, and Sam ducked down to catch her gaze.

"You think I shouldn't?" A mixture swirled in Sam's stomach, one part apprehension, two parts bitterness. Was her best friend against her goals now, too? She couldn't do this alone. Cole might be on her side, but even that was mostly because he was as tired of the dude ranch as Sam was and wanted a way out.

Kate finally looked up to meet her eyes. "I think you should do what you feel is right. But I would rather Jenson Farms go under than you get hurt or…" Her voice trailed off but Sam didn't have to wonder where Kate's train of thought headed. Sam's own thoughts chugged toward the exact same place every time she mounted Lucy.

"I know my dad died riding a bull. And the irony of it happening at the same annual rodeo I'm entering isn't lost on me. But I have to do this. For him. For the ranch." Sam bit her lower lip. "For myself."

"Then do it." Kate leaned over and squeezed Sam's arm. "I believe in you."

Sudden emotion pricked Sam's eyes and she swallowed the hard lump rising in her throat. "I'm glad someone does."

They sat in companionable silence, then Kate jumped to her feet. "We can't be mushy without brownies. You want one? I made them this afternoon."

"Sure." Sam joined Kate in the red-accented kitchen and got a plate out of the cabinet. She knew the details of the house as well as Kate did by now, after all the time they'd spent here since Kate's purchase almost two years ago. As happy as Sam was for her friend, she couldn't help the finger of envy that poked her side every now and then. Of course she was glad Kate had her own place, but Sam wanted freedom, too. Not away from Jenson Farms, necessarily, but away from the stress of chores, money, obligation.

In essence, her life.

Kate scooped a giant brownie onto Sam's plate. "Big enough?"

"For now." Sam bit into the chocolate bar. "Perfect."

"Speaking of perfect." Kate's eyebrows wiggled as she chomped into her own brownie. "What do you think of Daniel?"

A wedge of brownie lodged in Sam's throat and she bent over double, coughing. Kate pounded her on the back. "I guess that's my answer."

"No," Sam croaked. She took the bottle of water Kate snagged from the fridge door and gulped a mouthful. "Went down the wrong pipe."

"So you don't have a problem with Daniel?" The hope in Kate's eyes made the snack churn in Sam's stomach. "He seems interested in me. I know it's a little far-fetched—he could have any woman he wanted—but I think he's sincere."

Sam brushed at a crumb on her mouth to stall for time. What could she say? That Daniel seemed like a complete sleazeball? That he came across more focused on money and impressions than anything else? That there was an obvious wedge between him and Ethan that Sam couldn't yet explain? She had no proof to offer other than her instincts. But if Sam warned Kate off Daniel now, she'd look jealous after having just confessed she'd made a fool of herself in front of Ethan. Sam refused to lose the only support she had left.

She raised her brownie to her lips and said the only honest

thing she could. "Daniel Ames would be a fool not to like you, Kate." Then she bit into her chocolate dessert before she could add any more truth to her statement.

Ethan couldn't look in the mirror. Every time he did, the image staring back disgusted him. No wonder his father always tried to teach him to keep his personal life and professional life separate. When mixed, they proved combustible.

And someone was about to get burned.

He splashed water on his face, blurring the reflection, and turned away from the bathroom sink. It might be too late already, if his heart had anything to say about it. The first time Sam turned that wildflower-blue gaze on him, he should have known this would happen. How could he have ever thought it'd be okay to keep the truth from her?

His father must be a better teacher than Ethan thought.

Ethan snatched the hand towel from its metal hook. The material snagged a loose piece of paneling on the wall, and he quickly tugged it free. That was the second time that week. He should mention it to Sam to have it fixed before he or the next guests occupying this particular cabin scratched themselves on it.

He quickly wiped his face dry with the torn towel. It wasn't too late. He could go to Sam right now, confess his real profession and why he was on the ranch, tell her he wanted nothing to do with his parents' schemes, and hope she'd forgive him.

But the confession still wouldn't be entirely true. Ethan didn't want to manipulate Sam's family, but how could he please both Sam and his father at the same time? Ethan might be ready to step out from the family business of his own accord, but he was no where near ready to be pushed away—emotionally or financially.

Maybe his father would just claim Daniel as his son instead, and Ethan would finally be replaced in every aspect of his parents' lives. Why not make it official when that's where Jeffrey Ames's loyalties seemed to rest, anyway?

Bitterness coated Ethan's tongue and he reached for his toothbrush, even though he'd already brushed his teeth once that evening. He'd scrub them all night if that meant avoiding lying sleeplessly in bed, contemplating how he'd ever get out of the pit he'd dug for himself. Sure, he could blame his dad for some of the shovelfuls of dirt, maybe Daniel for a few others, but Ethan was a grown man. Despite feeling caged in all his life, he still ultimately made his own choices.

And right now, he had to decide if finally gaining his father's love and respect was worth losing Sam's heart forever.

He could push aside his feelings for Sam, and commit to getting the cheapest price possible on the Jensons' ranch—just as Jeffrey Ames hoped. Only he would go about it honestly, not by means of manipulation. That choice would bring money, the chance for eventual independence from the real estate business, and better yet, it would show his father that Ethan was successful and worthy of respect. And maybe Sam could start over somewhere and be happy.

Or he could be honest with Sam. Tell her the truth and accept the consequences. But that choice would bring only division between her and her mother for the kept secrets, anger at Ethan for being deceitful, and would permanently destroy any chance Ethan had of convincing her he could be worthy of her love.

Ethan left the bathroom and sank on his bed in the cabin. It was early still in the evening, but fatigue clung to the edges of his frayed emotions, coaxing him toward sleep. Daniel's bed remained empty, typical for a Friday night. He was probably at the lodge again. Thankfully, they hadn't spoken much since the fair the night before. Ethan wasn't sure what he would tell his cousin if he broached the subject of the carnival. Encourage Daniel toward Kate in hopes of convincing him to back off the pursuit of Sam? Or just step back and see what would happen naturally?

Ethan flopped back against the bed pillows and closed his eyes, not even bothering to take off his shoes. He was tired of feeling as if his entire life was controlled by his father. Tired of being stuck between choices too hard to make. But most of all, he was tired of his conscience complicating his life.

It'd be so much easier if his moral radar would quit getting in the way. Why couldn't he just be heartless like his dad and Daniel? It was more than simply being attracted to Sam that made him think twice before following Jeffrey's orders. It was the entire way his family ran the business. Underhanded schemes, manipulation, shortcuts. When Ethan first joined the company years ago, he was too young and naive to grasp what was happening behind the scenes, until he and Daniel took over the real estate side of the business. By then, it was easier to keep up the heartless rich guy charade that Daniel naturally mastered than demand answers or ethics from his parents.

But a man could only live off the superficial for so long.

Ethan's eyes opened and slowly adjusted to the dim light of the cabin. Evening shadows fell through the partially open miniblinds, draping his dresser and bedside table in darkness. Night was approaching, and in a few short hours, Sam would be in the paddock practicing on Lucy. He would go watch, be supportive, and try to find a way to keep her safe. It would only be a matter of time before Daniel told Jeffrey about Sam's plans to win the needed money for that stallion. Daniel was probably just waiting for the opportune time that would make him look the best. Ethan never once thought he'd be fighting with his cousin for the same girl.

Then again, he never thought he'd be falling for a cowgirl, either.

Chapter Sixteen

Ethan arrived at the paddock just in time to see Sam slam hard onto the dirt-packed earth. Lucy trotted away, but Sam remained motionless on the ground. "Sam!" Ethan's heart thundered louder than a horse's galloping hooves as he ran toward the pen, a prayer leaving his lips for the first time in he didn't know how long. He scaled the fence, nearly colliding with Cole, who already knelt by Sam. Ethan dropped to the dirt beside him, out of breath. "Is she all right?" *Please, God. She's the one bit of good I still have in my life.*

"I don't know." Barely contained panic masked Cole's face as he gently touched Sam's cheek. "You okay, kid?"

The full moon made her stark features seem even paler against the deep brown of the dirt. Ethan fought the urge to grab Sam and shake her. She had to be okay. Why wasn't she moving? His breath hitched.

"Kid?" Cole's voice wavered.

Sam slowly opened her eyes, then blinked repeatedly. "What happened?"

"You fell off Lucy again." Cole rocked back on his booted

heels, forearms pressed against his jean-clad knees. He lowered his head and inhaled deeply. “You scared us for a second there.”

Relief flooded Ethan’s senses as Sam struggled to sit up. He gripped her arm to help. Sam winced and reclined back in the dirt. “Maybe I’ll just stay here a minute.”

The worry returned to Cole’s face and he hovered over her once more. “You need a doctor.”

“No!” The harsh word shot from Sam’s mouth like a bullet from a rifle. “I’m just sore. Nothing’s broken.”

“Are you sure?” Cole studied the length of Sam’s body. “Move your legs.”

She complied, somewhat reluctantly, Ethan could see by the frustrated expression on her face.

“Now your arms.”

Sam wiggled her arms at both sides.

“Neck.”

She rotated it easily around her shoulders.

“Pinky toes.”

“What?” Sam sat up, brow pinched. “How could that possibly matt—”

Cole grinned and Ethan let loose the smile he’d been holding once he caught on to Cole’s game.

Sam’s eyes narrowed at them both. “Very funny.” She rubbed her elbows with both hands, smearing dirt up her bare forearms.

Cole shrugged. “Just lightening the mood. But you’re sitting now, aren’t you?” He stood and offered his hand to pull Sam to her feet.

Ethan stood with them, the residue of fear still weakening his legs. That had been close—too close. Sam was crazy to want to do this. There had to be a different way for her to earn some substantial cash. Either she was clueless as to what that other option was—or another secret lurked that she hadn't told him yet.

"I'm going to put Lucy up for the night." Cole gripped Sam's shoulder. "Holler if you need anything, you hear?" He turned to Ethan without waiting for an answer. "Watch her for me." He then jogged toward the other end of the paddock after Lucy.

"I don't need a nanny." Sam rested her weight against the fence and slid down to a sitting position against the middle rail. She leaned over and braced her head in her hands.

"Good thing, because I'm a horrible babysitter." Ethan inched down beside her, reaching for her shoulder but withdrawing his hand before he could make contact. She deserved better than concocted sympathy. But somehow he knew his feelings were no longer fake. Not if the full-blown panic he'd felt moments ago was any indication. He hesitated, and then rested his hand lightly on the dirty, rolled-up sleeve of her shirt. "Why are you doing this, Sam?"

At his touch, Sam looked up, but her eyes didn't seem quite focused. She stared somewhere over his shoulder, as if privately viewing an invisible shadow far away. Ethan turned but the only thing behind them was open pasture, fields of sage green turned silver in the moonlight.

"My dad died riding a bull."

The words fell from Sam's lips like a buried confession and the weight of their meaning pressed into Ethan's chest. He drew a constricted breath. "When?"

"Two years ago." Sam arched her spine, pressing both hands into the small of her back. She winced, undoubtedly sore from her fall. "At the Appleback rodeo."

"The same one you're entering." The brunt of her situation hit Ethan then, clenching his heart like a brutal fist. No wonder she'd bristled at his comment of being trampled the other night. How insensitive could he be?

Ethan's earlier decision to persevere with the pursuit of the sale, regardless of the consequences to Sam, disintegrated before his eyes. Sam couldn't ride in the rodeo—not because of the potential of winning the prize money and preventing the Ameses from buying her farm—but because in that moment, Ethan knew he couldn't handle losing her. It was too dangerous. Seeing Sam landing in the dirt like that, inches from Lucy's horns and hooves, was more than he could handle.

Sam continued on as if she hadn't just verbally and emotionally drop-kicked Ethan in the stomach. "Dad was a big star when I was younger." She smiled, still staring into the distance as if she could still clearly view her father across the pasture. "He used to toss his cowboy hat in the air after each winning ride. It was his trademark. Then he'd point to my mom and me in the stands and wink. He always called me his Rodeo Sweetheart, back when I barrel-raced. That's Appleback's unofficial title for a female competitor who wins their category."

Sam's grin faded and the night breeze tossed a strand of her light hair across her cheeks. Ethan tucked it behind her ear.

"Dad quit the circuit for us." Her lips pressed together and tears filled her eyes. "Because it was dangerous."

"Then what happened?" Ethan's fingers trailed down her arm to gently squeeze her hand. Sam clung to his grip, clearly lost in memory. Somehow, painful as it was, Ethan had the feeling Sam needed to share this as much for her own benefit as for his.

"He was invited back for a hometown tribute, here in Appleback where his fame began. The crowd wanted him to ride one more time, show off for them. He did it, even though my mom told him he shouldn't." Sam shuddered. "He was trampled. Spent the last few weeks of his life in a hospital bed surrounded by a bunch of machines, all of them beeping, teasing us with the hope that he'd pull through."

"I'm so sorry." Ethan's words sounded hollow to his own ears, completely useless, but what else could he say? He sat in silence, mourning with her for a man he didn't even know but could safely assume must have been special to have turned out a daughter like Sam. What would it have been like to have such a close relationship with his dad? He couldn't even picture it. In regards to emotion or affection, his father was as good as dead, too. Only pride and power flowed through Jeffrey Ames's veins. Not love.

An empty spot inside Ethan opened then, a fresh wound he'd worked for years to scab over. It ripped apart, bleeding regret into the dry places of his heart. If his own father passed away, would Ethan even miss him? He swallowed hard. He couldn't pursue that thought now, not when Sam was about to make the same mistake her father did. "Don't do it, Sam. Don't ride."

Sam's blue gaze searched his, studying, seeking, full of restrained emotion. Her lips parted to answer, but Ethan pressed on, seizing the last opportunity he might ever get to change her mind. He could hear the desperation in his voice but couldn't restrain it. "Let me help you instead. We can work something out. It wouldn't be charity, I promise. Whatever it takes."

She tilted her head, eyes narrowing in thought. Ethan held his breath. She was considering it. Was there a chance she'd finally listen to reason?

Across the paddock, the chute gate banged open. Ethan jumped. Several yards away, Cole led Lucy from the makeshift stall into the shadows of the field near the barn. Ethan turned back to Sam but the moment was lost, that thoughtful gaze now replaced by a determined sheen.

Sam stood and squared her shoulders. "I have to do this." She crossed the paddock, the rigid line of her back further punctuating her statement, her dirt-covered clothes testimony of her resolve. Then she half turned with a scowl. "With or without your support."

Sam strode away from Ethan, fists clenched, wishing her boots were long enough to kick herself. She couldn't believe she'd almost let him get to her that way. She'd been *that* close to agreeing not to ride in the rodeo—and for what? Because he'd looked at her so pleadingly? Because his eyes held a hint of romanticism she'd only read about in books? She'd never been the type of girl to fall for such a ploy, and the fact that she nearly had scared her more than bull riding.

She yanked open the door to the house and remembered just in time not to clomp up the stairs. She pulled off her boots and tip-toed up the steps to her room, holding her breath as she passed Angie's door. At least Sam had jerked back to her senses with Cole slamming the gate behind Lucy like he did. Otherwise, who knew what she'd have agreed to? *Yes, Ethan, I'll drop out of the rodeo for you. Sure, Ethan, I'll run away with you.* Sam scoffed. Right. Like he'd even offer.

Would you want him to?

Her traitorous thoughts mocked her as Sam locked herself in her room and reached for her pajamas in the top dresser. She didn't know what she wanted anymore. The idea of someone arriving to save the day used to sound like a cop-out, a cheesy notion meant only for helpless females in romance novels and low-budget movies. But now, the notion seemed to carry more relief than annoyance. It'd be nice to have the burden of money fall on more capable shoulders for once. Her own were sunburned, bruised and beyond weary.

A verse she'd memorized as a child in Sunday school came to mind as Sam threw back the covers on her bed. *Come unto me, all ye that labour and are heavy laden, and I will give you rest.*

Rest. What a concept. Some days it felt like Sam wouldn't recognize rest if it jumped up and grabbed her around the neck. She slipped between the cool sheets and buried her head in her pillow, the verse still rolling around in her mind. She wished her family hadn't been forced to stop attending services regularly in order to run the ranch, or maybe she'd have found some comfort for their current circumstances in the fellowship there.

She rolled over onto her back, turning her head away from the glowing alarm clock numbers. *All ye that labour and are heavy laden.* At least she fit the description required for help. With the exception of her mother and maybe Cole, Sam didn't think anyone in the city of Appleback could fulfill the prerequisite better. God could take away her burdens, but she had the sneaking feeling He wanted to help her through them instead.

In between snippets of "heels down" and "chin up," her father had often talked about God. Mini life lessons mixed in with the riding instruction. "God's not a genie, Sam. When you ask Him for something, it better not be selfish."

A nostalgic smile turned Sam's lips. The advice hadn't stopped her for praying every night for a gold buckle in barrel racing, but it sure helped her appreciate it more when she finally earned it. She was the only girl in the competition who told everyone God had helped her win.

A tear slipped from the corner of Sam's eye and trailed into her ear. When her father died, she'd lost that childlike passion for her faith along with the passion for life. She still believed in God, of course, and knew better than to push Him away, too. His comforting arms helped her survive the aftermath of her father's passing, but sometime after that, she'd grown distant, developed the age-old attitude of "God helps those who helps themselves." She set out to help herself, all right, and what had that gotten her? A ranch in the red and a lonely existence.

A weight settled on Sam's chest, pressing her burden even heavier onto her shoulders. She flopped on her side and wiped at her wet cheeks. She really was only a crumbling shell of what she'd once been. Her dad wouldn't have wanted her to stop living just because he did—so why had she?

Maybe this rodeo would be more cathartic than she'd first thought. Not only could she win the money to save the ranch, but she could honor her father's memory. Maybe then the pain would lessen just a little, and she could finally move on with her life.

Despite Ethan's attempts at persuading her otherwise, Sam had to ride. It was more important than ever. If she didn't, not only would her chances of buying Noble Star disappear, but she feared, so would her very spirit.

Sam closed her eyes, begging sleep to come. To erase the physical memory of landing in the dirt just hours before. To erase the recording of Ethan's coaxing, pleading voice now looping in her head on repeat. But most of all, to erase the imprint of fire his gentle touch on her arm seemed to brand into her skin.

Ethan Ames, handsome or not, was nothing but trouble for a woman with a goal such as hers. Sam had no time to wait around and be rescued, and unless God intervened, she would have to once again save the day herself.

And if one day some prince offered to sweep Sam off her feet, he sure as shootin' better be more of a cowboy than Ethan Ames.

Chapter Seventeen

Ethan clicked his tongue at Wildfire, urging him forward from the stall. The horse grudgingly followed, hay dangling from his thick lips. Regardless of the gelding's voracious appetite, it was time for the Saturday-morning ride, and Sam already had her hands full tacking up the remaining horses in the paddock. Cole had stumbled into the arena minutes earlier with a stuffy nose and fever, so Sam immediately sent him away with strict instructions to take medicine, chug a glass of water and drift back to sleep. It looked like the trail ride was up to Ethan and Sam to handle now. Hopefully the stable hand would be better by tomorrow night to help with the bonfire cookout Sam had been looking forward to for days.

He blinked against the sun as he stepped out of the barn, Wildfire close behind. Ethan's mom was lined up outside with the other guests, along with the honeymoon couple he'd seen at the lodge the other night. Unfortunately, so were Mike and Davy. The father was talking to Angie Jenson—as usual, it seemed—and Davy was attempting to scale the adjacent paddock fence where the stallions grazed, despite his father's repeated protests. Ethan groaned. Figured that the one day they were shorthanded, the terrible twosome decided to show up.

He looped Wildfire's lead rope around the fence post, then his hands stilled over the frayed material. When had he started considering himself part of the staff? He shook his head. Those thoughts would only get him in trouble. Ethan might be participating in chores—and there was no arguing he'd learned a lot over the past week or so—but Sam made it clear that was as far as it went. Would he ever be able to impress her?

And would it ever stop mattering so much whether or not he did?

Across the rail, Sam looked up from saddling Piper and offered a short nod in Ethan's direction. He smiled in return, but she kept her eyes on the task in front of her. Hopefully she was just busy and not holding a grudge against his attempts last night at talking her out of the rodeo. Time would tell if she was mad, that much was certain—with Sam, her feelings were right there on her shirtsleeve along with the tiny red checked pattern.

He should have known she wouldn't have gone for dropping out. But in that one moment in time, he had really thought she might consider it. He just couldn't get comfortable with the idea of Sam risking her life, no matter how worthy the cause.

Ethan secured Wildfire's rope with a quick yank. He wondered what would happen if he bought the Stephenses' coveted stallion for Sam? Called Kate's father, swore him to secrecy, handed over the money—even if it did have to come from his savings—and plopped the horse right there in the paddock, along with the other stallions left over from the Jensons' breeding farm days? She'd never know who did it.

He risked a glance at Sam from the corner of his eye. Yeah, right. Not only would Sam know immediately who'd bought the horse, she'd make Ethan take it back. The only thing firmer than her no-charity rule would be Jeffrey's tone as he threatened Ethan's job—and his place in the family. Talk about the extreme other end of an order. Ethan was supposed to be talking Sam out of entering the rodeo—not offering to make the path easier. *God, a little advice would be greatly appreciated.* Ever since his desperate prayer last night at seeing Sam fall, talking to God had suddenly become easy for the first time in years. Ethan wasn't sure what had changed, but for now, he was rolling with it. It felt good being back on speaking terms.

"Wildfire's ready to be tacked up." Ethan patted the gelding's neck as he ducked underneath to edge closer to Sam. "What can I do next?" At least helping out around the ranch made the guilt that seemed to keep permanent residence in his throat easier to swallow.

Sam straightened from tugging at the saddle's girth strap and brushed a damp strand of hair off her forehead. "If you could saddle Wildfire, I'll bring Diego from the barn. Then we should be ready to ride."

"No problem." Ethan slid the blanket on top of Wildfire's back as Sam hurried toward the stables. He couldn't keep from watching her leave, despite his attempts to focus on the buckles in his hand. Did Sam have any idea how beautiful she was? The girls from his regular group of friends in New York would clamor for their compacts and hairbrushes the second they began to perspire—yet Sam would work up a flat-out sweat in this Texas heat and do nothing other than mop her brow with her shirtsleeve and keep working. That kind of confidence was so much more attractive than the superficial beauty of his old crowd.

Ethan frowned as he straightened the blanket and reached for Wildfire's saddle. Old crowd, as in past tense? This working vacation was messing up his mindset in more ways than one. In a matter of days, he had to go back to New York with his family—to his old life, even if only for a short time while he prepared for his new one. He was getting far too attached to Sam—and to the slower pace of Texas, for that matter. Even the southern accents were growing on him. What would it be like to relocate somewhere with a drawl? Somewhere with grass as far as the eye could see, instead of skyscrapers?

A sudden high-pitched scream split the air, followed by a distressed whinny. Ethan spun around. The trouble-making boy, Davy, had managed to slip inside the stallions' fence and now was trapped between two skittish horses. The terror on the kid's face sprung Ethan into action. He dropped the saddle and bolted toward the paddock.

"Davy!" Mike yelled. His face turned white and he rushed the fence, Angie right behind him.

"Grab him, Mike!"

Sam emerged from the barn, her confused expression a blur as Ethan sped past her. "Come on!"

She immediately sprinted behind him, her booted footsteps thudding in Ethan's wake. Mike had climbed inside the paddock but still couldn't reach his son. One of the stallions reared, clipping Mike's shoulder with his hooves. He crumpled to the ground.

Sam and Ethan reached the fence at the same time. She reached beneath the rails for Mike and grabbed his arms, pulling him away from the danger and into the grass beside the paddock. Angie stooped to help, and Ethan vaulted over the top rail into the pen.

One of the stallions snorted in Ethan's direction and pawed

the ground. "Davy, very slowly, come around the horse to my side." He kept his voice even and tried to smile. No doubt the horses were sensing Davy's fear and reacting accordingly. It wouldn't help adding his own anxiety into the mix. Was Mike okay? Hopefully the throng of horses had blocked Davy's view of seeing his dad fall.

Davy, eyes wide and teary, took a half step toward Ethan, but was still boxed in between the disgruntled horses. Ethan nodded. "You're doing good. Keep going."

Then suddenly the brown stallion blocking Davy's path reared up on his hind legs. Ethan snatched Davy's shirt collar and hauled the kid toward the fence before the horse could land. The force slammed them both against the paddock. Better that than falling under the anxious animal's hooves.

Ethan helped Davy scramble back over the rails before quickly doing the same. The stallions tossed their heads, ears pinned flat, but seemed relieved to have the sudden intruders gone from their territory.

Davy flew to his father's side. Mike sat up slowly and groaned. "Daddy, are you okay?"

"Yes, are you?" Mike touched his son's head as if checking for injuries, then pulled him into a tight hug.

"That was a close one." Sam stood from her kneeling position and shoved her hair back from her face with both hands. Relief peppered her expression.

Angie brushed her hands on her jeans and turned an admiring gaze on Ethan. "Well done. The horses really responded to you."

"That's funny. They looked terrified to me." Ethan released the breath he hadn't realized he'd been holding. That *had* been close—too close.

"Red, the bigger of the horses in there, would have had no

problem dancing all over you and Davy if he was scared enough to do so." Angie tucked her hair behind her ears. "You calmed him down. Very impressive."

Ethan cleared his throat. "If I had known Red was such a beast I might not have been so effective." He didn't deserve the attention, he'd just happened to be closest to the situation at the time. It wasn't like he'd jumped from a burning building. He was all too aware of his exceeding lack of superpowers—Jeffrey and Daniel served as a constant reminder of that.

"I just hope a certain young man has learned his lesson." Mike clapped Davy's shoulder as they both slowly stood to their feet. "Isn't that right?"

Davy nodded his agreement and Ethan could barely contain his snort. Hopefully the boy's father would learn a similar lesson in paying attention. If Mike had kept his son corralled instead of flirting with Angie, this wouldn't have happened.

Although Angie didn't seem to mind the attention. She ushered the twosome toward the main house. "We better get some ice on your shoulder, Mike."

"I guess we can get on with the morning ride, then." Sam let out her breath. Her gaze locked with Ethan and he couldn't help smiling at the admiration lingering in her eyes. Maybe he'd finally impressed her after all.

There just might be more cowboy in Ethan than she originally thought. Sam ambled along on Diego, the warm sun lulling her thoughts far away from the trail ride at hand—and straight toward Ethan riding just a few paces away. She couldn't help being impressed at his rescue of Davy. Ethan hadn't thought twice before rushing into the stallions' pen to save the boy. That showed courage above fear—definite cowboy traits. He'd also had the instinct to stay relaxed and try to calm the horses without further panicking them or Davy. Then, on top of all that, he tried to disregard the praise he'd earned, had even looked a little embarrassed by it. That proved he hadn't done it all for show, but to truly help.

Apparently starched shirts and gold-tipped pens didn't hide character as much as Sam first thought.

She absently brushed a fly from Diego's mane. Sam certainly didn't know any city slickers who would have done what Ethan did back there. It was beginning to look as if she wouldn't be able to use that unofficial label anymore.

She also couldn't keep clinging to the anger that kept her up last night. Despite Ethan's trying to talk her out of the rodeo, it was growing harder and harder to stay mad. He was just looking out for her. Annoying, maybe—but sweet. A far cry from the calloused greenhorn that showed up at the ranch just a few weeks ago. Who knew what soft layer Ethan would reveal next?

Sam urged Diego forward on the trail, his long tail flicking from side to side and tickling the back of her arms. It was actually easier being around Ethan when he played the sarcastic, teasing jerk like when he first arrived, insisting on using her full name and expecting special treatment. This mature, considerate—and masculine—version was far too attractive for Sam's own good.

A few yards ahead, Ethan twisted around in the saddle and glanced back at her, as if reading her thoughts. Sam ducked her head but couldn't keep her traitorous gaze from catching his own once again. He smiled and her stomach shivered, just like last year when she rode the Gravy Train at the fair and began to descend the highest hill.

Sam swallowed hard and looked away. She was falling, all right.

* * *

"It's Saturday night. No hot date?" Angie grinned from the loveseat in the den as Sam attempted to climb the stairs to her room. Her mother was always trying to encourage her to have more of a social life.

Sam paused on the bottom step, muscles stiff with fatigue and too much exercise. She should have stretched more before riding Lucy last night—not that any amount of preparation could have softened that particular fall. Plus, the at-home exercises Cole had Sam doing left her abs permanently sore, and all the time she spent in the saddle today hadn't helped. She forced a smile, hoping her mom wouldn't notice her discomfort. "I don't think I've ever had a hot date, Mom." For some reason, the words brought Ethan to the forefront of her mind and Sam shook her head to dislodge them.

"You always did prefer horses over boys." Angie smiled. "A fact that had your father elated. But I want you to be able to go out and enjoy life and not get so bogged down by the farm." She sipped from her oversize mug. "Clara made a fresh pot of coffee before she left for the evening. It's still hot if you want some."

Sam started to say no. After all, it'd be a long day of chores and tourists, and she had only a few hours to sleep before meeting Cole and Lucy again. Reminiscing about the past—boys or her dad—was not at the top of her to-do list. But something hollow and wistful in her mother's expression changed her mind. She sighed. "Sure, why not?"

Sam prepared her coffee and sank onto the couch opposite her mom, nestling back against the cushions. "How's Davy after the near accident this morning?"

"He's fine. Mike is too." Angie gave her a pointed look over the rim of her mug. "They're a little shaken up, but okay."

"Maybe if Mike spent more time watching his son than watching—" The words stuck in Sam's mouth and she quickly swallowed them with her coffee. The hot liquid burning her tongue was more tolerable than the heated expression on her mom's face.

Angie frowned. "Watching what?"

Sam lowered her cup. "You. Mom, don't pretend Mike doesn't follow you around like a lovesick puppy."

"Oh, he does not," Angie scoffed, but something that looked a lot like amusement, even delight, lit her eyes.

"He does, too. He's interested, which is pathetic because he must think you're married." She gestured to the ring on her mother's left finger.

"He knows about your father." Angie's voice softened and she studied the glittering diamond on her hand. "We've talked about it before. He also knows I'm not ready to take this off yet."

Relief filled Sam's stomach and she set her coffee down, suddenly full. If her mom wasn't ready to take off the ring, then there was no immediate danger of her getting serious with another man—especially Mike. Sam's nose wrinkled. That'd be too many changes at once. No, one problem at a time. Saving the ranch came first, then finding love.

For both of them.

"But you know Sam, one day, we'll have to move on." Angie's eyes met hers as she leaned over to set her mug on the coffee table. "Your father wouldn't have wanted either of us to waste our lives."

He also wouldn't have wanted Mike anywhere near her mom, but Sam imagined this wasn't the best time to make such a statement. She nodded, lips pressed tight.

"One day you're going to need a life of your own." Angie rubbed her hands over her cheeks. "Sometimes I wonder if

I'm putting too much pressure on you, keeping you here to work instead of making your own career, your own path. You just said yourself you don't even have time to date."

"Mom, no. Don't think that." Sam leaned forward. "It's my choice. Sometimes I get overwhelmed with the load we carry, but that's not your fault. You didn't wish for any of this."

"But I want you to have fun, too." The words came out a whisper and Angie looked away, fiddling with her ring. "You know, I hate to push you into something you don't want, but maybe selling the ranch, starting over would be good for us. Give both of us a fresh start."

Sam sucked in her breath. "But this is our home. This is all we have left of Dad."

"That's why I haven't." Angie sighed. "Yet."

"Mom, don't be silly. We'll make it through this. You're just stressed about our finances. Things will get better soon." Fresh determination to win the rodeo filled Sam's heart and she stood up, arms out to hug her mom. "You'll see."

"I hope you're right, baby," Angie hugged her back, arms tight against her neck. "I hope you're right."

Chapter Eighteen

The bonfire crackled and hissed, orange sparks shooting into the night air for a brief moment of glory before slowly extinguishing on a gust of wind. Ethan held a metal clothes hanger over the flames and rotated the marshmallow dangling from the end. He snuck another look at Sam, laughing on the other side of the stacked wood with Angie and a few other guests. Her face, illuminated by the glow of the flames, shone with happiness as she tilted her head back and laughed.

Ethan's grip on the hanger and his stomach tightened simultaneously. He'd thought she was beautiful before, but when she laughed—wow. He tried to look away but his eyes didn't want to obey. Sam glanced over and met his gaze, and her smile slowly faded from laughter to a private grin, just between the two of them. She whispered something to her mom and then stood and made her way around the bonfire.

His stomach flipped again as Sam settled onto the log bench beside him. He opened his mouth to say hi but his tongue suddenly resembled sawdust. What did that little smile mean? Did she feel the connection between them, too? Their own personal flame—

"Ethan? Your marshmallow is black."

He jerked his eyes back to the fire and winced. His once puffy marshmallow now looked like a hardened ball of charcoal. "Must have gotten distracted." He lobbed it off into the fire and reached for a new one from the plastic bag at his feet.

"Distracted by what?" Sam's shoulder brushed his as she held out her hand for the bag.

Their fingers touched as he handed her the marshmallows and this time he knew there was no hiding the reaction on either of their faces. He held on to the bag, refusing to relinquish the small bit of contact. "Sam, I—"

"Listen up, everyone!" Angie stood by the fire and clapped her hands.

Ethan jumped, and Sam's hand slipped from his grasp. She drew a tight breath before turning her eyes to her mother. Ethan reluctantly did the same. *Great timing, Mrs. Jenson.*

"We're glad we had such a good turnout for our bonfire tonight. I'm happy you're all enjoying yourselves." She brushed her hair out of her eyes as a gust of evening wind teased the fire. "If you want another hot dog, there are leftovers on the card table by the oak tree. Marshmallows are being passed around now, and extra hangers are on that line over there. Hurry up and eat, because the games are about to begin." She smiled before settling back onto the log seat by Mike.

Davy sat beside his father, uncommonly quiet as he cooked a marshmallow on a hanger. Maybe the incident with the stallions had finally calmed the kid. Ethan had never wanted children before, and Davy's recent behavior only confirmed that fact. Yet looking at Sam, he couldn't help but wonder if their kids would have her wavy, light-colored hair and blue eyes or his darker looks.

Ethan quickly reined in that thought process. He was

moving way too fast, even in his own mind. Sam hadn't been sharing a secret smile earlier, she was laughing at him for burning the marshmallow while staring into space—staring at her. He'd better back off before what was in his heart became too obvious on the outside.

"Your mom looks like she's having a good time." Sam pointed across the camp fire. Vickie sat by Daniel and was trying to trap a marshmallow between two chocolate-covered graham crackers to make a s'more. The marshmallow oozed over the sides onto the plate and she laughed, swiping the excess on Daniel's arm.

"She sure does." Ethan's heart flinched at the easy camaraderie his mom had with his cousin. Once again, he was out of the loop. Some things never changed. What was it about Daniel that his parents preferred? His cut-throat business savvy? His willingness to do what the job took, regardless of the negative consequences to innocent people? Ethan didn't want to be like that—but what if that was the only way to ever earn his parents' affection and respect?

Was it worth it?

"I'm surprised your father isn't here." Sam plucked a marshmallow from the bag and skewered it onto her hanger. "He hasn't participated in many of the ranch activities since you guys got here, though, has he?"

"No, he's not really into country life." The words slipped from Ethan's mouth before he could censor. Hopefully the night shadows would hide the lies he knew were plastered all over his expression. He turned his face away from the glow of the fire. If he couldn't look at himself in the mirror, no way could Sam see his eyes now. His family's entire cover would be blown in a second flat.

"Then why is he even here? I have to admit, when my

mom told me your family was coming and you were big-city VIPs, I wondered about it. I'd have guessed you'd hit up Europe or some exotic beach." Sam held her marshmallow over the fire, directly above where Ethan's burned one had fallen moments ago.

"We usually do." Ethan pressed his lips together and busied himself with another marshmallow. The sticky sweet stuck to his grimy fingers, black ash on white sugar. He dirtied everything he touched. But wasn't that why he was trying to get out of the business—to start a clean life? Yet the notion seemed impossible. There would always be one more lie to tell, one more web to weave before he was completely clear of the past—if he ever could be, with the last name Ames.

"What does your family do, anyway?" Sam bit into her roasted marshmallow, pieces of white crust clinging to her lips. She wiped her mouth with her hand but the sugar stuck there, too.

Ethan handed Sam a napkin from the pile someone had left beside him. The truth stuck in his throat and he coughed. What could he say that wouldn't be incriminating? Developers? Vague but still suspicious. Real estate? Definitely not. That'd be like waving a neon sign over his head. "We, uh…well, we—"

"Game time!" Angie jumped to her feet again, clanging a musical triangle. "We have a spotlight set up over there for horseshoes, and for those of you tired of the mosquitoes, in about thirty minutes there'll be a line-dance demonstration inside the lodge."

The crowd of guests immediately stood and began putting away their trash. Sam hopped up and brushed the dirt from her jeans. "Play horseshoes with me?" The anticipation lighting her eyes only further churned the hot dog in Ethan's stomach. He nodded and forced a smile in return.

Saved by the bell, Western-style.

Sam laughed and tugged the horseshoe from Ethan's hand. "No wonder they're flying over the fence. You're not holding them right." She held the horseshoe up so it resembled a backward C shape. "Grab it here, from the bottom. You want your fingertips to curl under the inside edge."

Ethan took the horseshoe and adjusted his grip. "Like this?"

"Yes, just keep your thumb on the flat side."

Ethan reared back and tossed the curved metal toward the tall pin staked in the ground. It landed at least three feet away. He winced. "I thought this was supposed to be an easy game."

"It can be, if you have any sense of direction or accuracy." Sam grinned.

"Very funny." Ethan shook the second horseshoe at her. "Let me guess. You're probably an expert and can play this blindfolded?"

She grabbed for the horseshoe but he held it just out of her reach. She bumped into his arm and he lifted the metal higher. "You're just afraid I'll show you up." She stretched for it again, jumping on her tiptoes.

"Ethan." Jeffrey Ames's deep voice boomed across the open field. Ethan stumbled backward a step away from Sam, his expression full of guilt as his dad drew closer. "We need to talk."

"Right now?" Ethan smiled, but it didn't quite reach his eyes. "I'm in the middle of a game."

"Right now." Jeffrey turned without acknowledging Sam and stalked up the slight hill toward the lodge, the breeze ruffling the sleeves of his dress shirt. Sam frowned. If Mr. Ames was on vacation, why didn't he participate in anything, or relax in comfortable clothing? If the country life wasn't his thing, as Ethan said, then why even come?

Her growing suspicion about the Ames family doubled and she shot Ethan a curious look. "What's that about?"

Ethan sighed and dropped the horseshoe on the ground. "Must be a business crisis. I'll meet you inside the lodge when we're done talking. I think your mom was right about the mosquitoes." He slapped at his arm as he hurried after Jeffrey.

Sam handed the horseshoe to another guest lining up to play, and started up the grassy incline toward the lodge. She might as well go inside and join the line-dance demonstration, and get her paranoid mind off Ethan and his family's motives. Just because Ethan had yet to tell her what he did for a living didn't mean anything was wrong. He probably just wanted to leave business behind while he was away from the office, and was frustrated because his dad wouldn't let him. That would make sense.

But the logic did nothing to quell the uneasy feeling in her stomach.

"When were you going to tell me about the girl's plans?" Jeffrey's eyebrows mashed into a thick line, the shadows surrounding the main house drawing harsh planes across his face. Music and laughter drifted from the lodge building next door.

Ethan checked over his shoulder to make sure Sam had continued to the lodge and wasn't within hearing distance. "What do you mean?"

"Don't play innocent with me. Daniel told me about the rodeo and the scheme to win enough money to buy some stallion." Jeffrey scowled. "What have you done to put a stop to this nonsense? She can't win the money, that would ruin everything."

"I know." Ethan rubbed his hands over the length of his face. "I've tried to talk her out of it, but she won't budge. She's determined to do this. It all goes back to her dad and his rodeo career—"

"I don't care if it goes back to Abe Lincoln. You have to stop it. If she wins the money, they might not have to sell the ranch." Jeffrey crossed his arms over his chest, gold cuff links glinting in the moonlight.

"I know, I'm trying—"

"Not hard enough." Jeffrey's eyes narrowed. "You act as if this sale has no benefit to you, no commission earned. What's the problem? I put you on this project, yet Daniel has been much more informative in less time."

Ethan's hands clenched into fists. "That's because you're playing him against me."

Jeffrey tilted his head to one side. "Is that what you think?"

"It's the truth, isn't it? Sending me on an errand just to have him pick up behind me."

Jeffrey glowered. "If you had your head on straight, you wouldn't need someone cleaning your mess. Now get back to that girl and stop her from entering that rodeo."

"Her name is Sam."

"Whatever. I want results, not personal attachment. I've taught you better than that." Jeffrey twisted the ring on his finger. "This ranch will be ours by the time we leave next week. Don't make me add *or else* to that statement."

Jeffrey stalked away before Ethan could reply, narrowly dodging another group of guests heading toward the lodge. Not that Ethan had a lot to say, other than the choice phrases running through his mind that he could never utter to his dad's face. Just because Jeffrey had zero respect for Ethan didn't mean he could be equally cruel back.

Ethan drew a deep breath, then headed for the lodge to meet Sam. Regardless of his dad's intrusion, he was determined to enjoy the rest of the evening with her.

For his own reasons, not his father's.

Chapter Nineteen

Twangy country music and the stomping of boots filled the lodge as Sam made her way inside. The furniture had been shoved against the walls to provide a dance floor, and guests happily twirled and two-stepped around the small space in time to the blaring stereo system. Sam poured herself a soda from the refreshment table in the back, grinning at a young couple who kept stepping on each other's feet. They laughed and teased, and the love radiating between them made Sam wish for something similar.

Longing lingered in Sam's throat after her first gulp of Coke. The conversation last night with her mother had only strengthened the emotions Sam tried to keep dormant. Would she ever have that kind of freedom and happiness? Thoughts of Ethan filled her mind and she quickly chugged the rest of her drink. It didn't matter. She had her priorities straight. Ranch first, love second—if ever.

"Want to dance?" Daniel appeared through the small crowd at Sam's side. "Come on, it'll be fun." He set down her cup and tugged her toward the dance floor before she could protest.

They joined the line of dancers, some with considerably more rhythm than others, and tried to fall into step. "This is my first time at a country dance, believe it or not," Daniel called over the music.

"Imagine that." Sam smiled but wished it were a different Ames man beside her. She slapped the back of each boot then turned a circle beside Daniel. "So are you enjoying your vacation?"

A confused expression crossed Daniel's face, then quickly faded. "Of course. The land is beautiful out here. I don't see much scenery like this in New York City." He winked before doing a slide-slide-step combo.

"You seemed to have hit it off with Kate." Sam tried to keep her voice casual. She wanted to know Daniel's motive for flirting with Kate, even though she figured it was nothing more serious than his flirting with her the same night—despite Kate wishing it to be more. "I know she had fun at the fair."

"I had fun, too." Daniel shrugged. "Gotta love a redhead." He winked again, and Sam wished she could poke something in his eye to keep it open.

"But you're not interested in her?"

The music faded away and a slow song on the CD took its place. Daniel held out his arms and Sam reluctantly allowed him to lead her. If not for trying to intervene on Kate's behalf, she would have made an excuse and fled back to the refreshment table. Even now, Daniel's cold, supersmooth hand on Sam's shoulder made her flinch. What did he do, moisturize every night before bed? Her hands were rougher than his.

"I enjoyed being around Kate." Daniel twirled Sam in a tight circle and pulled her back in. "But I enjoy being with you, too." A hidden agenda lit his dark eyes and Sam tugged from his grip.

"I should get—"

"Mind if I cut in?" Ethan stood behind Daniel, one hand firmly on his cousin's shoulder.

Relief flooded Sam's veins, and she eagerly moved toward Ethan. Daniel nodded once and stepped aside, but the expression on his face warned he wouldn't forget—or forgive—the interruption.

Ethan didn't seem to care. He gently took Sam in his arms and moved her around the dance floor with much more grace than Daniel had.

"I hope you don't mind. But if we can't finish our game of horseshoes, we can at least talk this way." Ethan smiled and Sam relaxed.

"I don't mind at all." Ethan's light touch on her shoulder proved his hands contained plenty of calluses now, and she smiled back. "What did your dad say? Is everything okay?"

Ethan stiffened beneath her arms, but kept swaying to the song. "Everything's fine. Just business talk."

"What kind of business?"

Ethan frowned. "Let's just enjoy the dance, okay? Talking about work is depressing."

"Do you not like what you do?" Sam tilted her head.

"I don't know." Ethan sighed. "Let's just say it's not what it started out as and leave it at that."

Sam opened her mouth with another question, then slowly pressed her lips together. It wasn't worth picking a fight over.

They kept dancing, the music building to a crescendo of violins and guitars, and she rested her head on Ethan's shoulder. His shirt was soft under her cheek and she closed her eyes, despite every instinct in her body warning her to retreat, to protect her heart, to run away. What was one dance?

The music enveloped them in a warm embrace, and Sam

squeezed her eyes shut. It was more than just a dance, and she knew it. It was a temporary escape, a hope for something that could never be. She was falling for one of her dreaded tourists, and falling fast. Even though Ethan had become so much more than the negative labels she'd so quickly branded on him, any chance of a relationship between them was doomed before it began. He was leaving, and she was staying. End of story.

"Samantha." Ethan's voice, low in her ear, jerked Sam from her thoughts.

Her heartbeat quickened but the familiar wave of indignation drowned out the momentary attraction. She stopped moving, forcing Ethan to a standstill. "I can't believe you called me that again."

"No, Sam, I—" Ethan rubbed his hands down his face, then exhaled sharply. His arms fell to his sides in defeat. "Look, I know you hate your name, but you're Samantha to me. You're so much more than tomboy Sam. You put on this front of being hardened, but I see the heart underneath. The soft, caring woman who has such deep love for her family, for honor, for animals. *That's* Samantha." He swallowed, his Adam's apple bobbing in his throat. "That's who I've come to care about more than I ever thought possible."

Sam stared at Ethan, the crowd of dancing guests around them blurring into a mix of swaying colors. Ethan cared about her? As more than a partnership, as more than a means of getting what he wanted by learning the ropes of a dude ranch? Impossible. Yet the thumping sensation in her stomach had nothing to do with the bass of the new song drumming from the speakers.

And everything to do with the man standing in front of her, arms open, heart exposed.

* * *

Ethan swallowed again, Sam's silence heavier than the crowd pressing around them. He waited, unwilling to risk more of his heart before she responded. Was she that disgusted with his confession? Or was she afraid to admit the same? He could only hope.

Not that it mattered. He was stirring up a violent nest by even voicing such thoughts. What could come of it other than heartache and conflict? Sam had no idea who his family was or what they did, despite her frequent questioning. He couldn't love her and keep such pertinent information from her, information that would destroy everything she was willingly sacrificing to have.

But he somehow did anyway.

"Samantha?" The name fell from his lips again, and this time her eyes closed in anguish.

"My dad called me Samantha." The pain in her expression slammed against Ethan like a Ferrari crashing into a tree. "No one has since he died."

"I'm so sorry. I didn't know." The hollow words sounded even emptier than he felt inside. He was a complete idiot. No wonder Sam was so defensive over her name. She didn't hate it or try to hide her identity behind a tough exterior—it was sentimental. Something special between her and her late father.

And he'd thrashed it like a horse's hooves galloping over a meadow.

"You couldn't have known." The agony slowly faded from Sam's eyes and she squeezed his hand. "I never told you. I just overreacted when you said it. It's my fault, too."

"You shouldn't have had to tell me. I should have respected your wishes from the start." Ethan laughed self-consciously. "Wow, I'm a real Romeo, aren't I?"

The serious expression returned to Sam's face and she looked over her shoulder. "Let's talk outside."

Ethan noticed the crowd thickening as a few couples meandered inside to escape the night air, and he nodded. "Good idea." He followed Sam outside, away from Davy and Mike still roasting marshmallows and laughing by the fire, and toward a quieter spot by the barn.

A horse's soft whinny broke the stillness of the night and Ethan leaned against the wall of the stables, trying to appear casual. Had Sam guided him here to confess her own feelings? Or to break his heart in private?

She stood in front of him, hands hooked in her front pockets. She looked down before finally meeting his gaze. "I know what you mean."

Hope straightened Ethan's shoulders. "You do?"

"Yes." Sam's eyes darted back to the ground. "But it doesn't matter."

"Why not?" But he knew the reason, knew it as surely as he knew the exact shade of Sam's eyes. The same reason he'd been screaming at himself the entire last week. Some lifestyles weren't meant to blend, theirs being an unfortunately prime example.

"For the same reason it would never work between Daniel and Kate." Sam exhaled loudly, the light of the moon above illuminating the contours of her face. Ethan tried not to fixate on the way the glow highlighted her delicate bone structure. She was even more beautiful by moonlight than by firelight, if that was possible. "We're too different. And you live across the country. And…" Her voice trailed off.

"And?" The word tasted like sawdust in his mouth. Not like they needed another reason but he wanted to hear it from Sam herself.

"And I don't know how much I can trust you."

The words, painfully true, took yet another shot at his heart and Ethan swallowed hard.

She lifted her thin shoulders in a helpless shrug. "We barely know each other. We have different morals, values, dreams."

"But you do feel the same." It came out a statement, not a question, and relief eased the wound on Ethan's hopes as Sam bit her lower lip and nodded.

His stomach tightened. He had to confess, had to tell her all. Regardless of the consequences, he couldn't keep up the charade a moment longer. He touched her arm. "Sam, I really—"

She tugged away, half turning her back to him as she stared up at the sky. "There's also the matter of your dad."

"What about him?" Ethan's hand fell slowly to his side, tingling with rejection.

"I've seen the way you talk to him, talk about him." Sam shook her head. "I know you have issues between you, that much is obvious, but it's not right. I would do anything to have two parents again." Her voice tightened and she sniffed.

Frustration mingled with the momentary dash of hope and his fist clenched. "You don't know anything about my family."

"And whose fault is that?" Sam's eyes snapped harder than her words.

"Trust me, you don't want to know our problems." Ethan wished he didn't have to know, either. Why couldn't he have been born into a family that valued each other more than money? If riches made people turn out like his father, he would rather drive a beat up car and shop at thrift stores for the rest of his life. He'd gladly trade the designer labels and the sports cars for even a week of unconditional love.

"I can't possibly imagine what kind of issue, business or otherwise, could make you two square off against each other like that. Father and son. It's ridiculous." Sam shook her head, her hair brushing against her cheeks. "Do you know how badly I wish my dad was here to argue with? When you've been in my position, your perspective changes. The trivial goes away, and you realize what's really important in life."

"Did you ever stop to consider that might be exactly what we fight about all the time?" Ethan backed away, his fists tightened into two knots.

"How could I know? Here you are confessing your feelings for me, yet you tell me nothing of your real life back in New York—and you expect me to respond with no hesitation?"

"Feelings you reciprocate."

Sam's mouth opened, and then snapped closed. Ethan tugged her toward him and her breath caught. "Tell me you don't."

She gulped, her eyes fixed on Ethan's lips. He darted his gaze to her mouth and then back to her eyes. She shook slightly under his grasp. "I can't."

Can't as in wouldn't? Or as in couldn't? It didn't matter. Ethan closed the remaining few inches between them and pressed his lips gingerly against hers. She stiffened in surprise before quickly returning his embrace. The kiss deepened and he cupped his hand at the back of her neck, easing her closer. She pulled away, breathless, and Ethan caught a whiff of wildflowers before she stumbled backward.

"I have to go." She touched her fingers to her lips, periwinkle eyes wide, before turning and slipping away into the shadows of the night.

Ethan collapsed against the barn wall, his heart pounding wildly in his chest. If he knew that was the way to win an argument with Sam, he'd have started a fight days ago.

Chapter Twenty

Sam's eyes fluttered open. She stared at the ceiling in her bedroom as the events of the previous night played in her head. Had it been a dream? She tugged her hand free of the sheets and felt her mouth. No, the kiss had been real. So had the argument, unfortunately.

She sighed as she rolled out of bed and turned off the alarm clock. For once she'd woken before the annoying blare, but the thoughts on repeat in her mind weren't any easier to listen to. Intrigue and regret chased circles around her heart as she dressed for work. Nice as the kiss had been, it didn't change her and Ethan's circumstances. If anything, it made them worse.

Sam pounded down the stairs into the kitchen. Too bad she couldn't leave her thought process behind as easily as her unmade bed. She snagged an apple from the fruit bowl at the counter. Clara stood by the kitchen sink, busy preparing breakfast for the guests. "Morning."

"Good morning." Clara dropped a dollop of biscuit dough on a cookie sheet. "I heard the party last night was a success."

Sam bit into her apple and wiped at her chin as heat flooded her face. "You could say that."

Clara stirred the dough before shaping another biscuit. "Good turnout?"

"Mmm-hmm." Sam chomped another bite, hoping her full mouth would discourage the topic.

But Clara shot a knowing look over her shoulder as she dusted her hands on the apron tied around her waist. "I also heard there was quite a commotion by the barn, around say ten-thirty?"

Sam stopped midchew. The kiss. She forced herself to swallow. "You're not—"

"Oh, goodness, no." Clara winked before grabbing the egg carton from the fridge. "I've never been one to gossip, but I think that other Ames boy doesn't live by the same policy."

Daniel. Sam closed her eyes. If he saw her and Ethan, and was already spreading the word, it wouldn't be long before her mother—

"Sam Jenson, I have a few questions for you." Angie's voice, firm and cold, sounded from the kitchen doorway.

She slowly turned. "I can explain."

"Explain why you were seen making out with a paying guest in public?" Angie crossed her arms over her chest, her brows knitted over narrowed eyes. "When I said I felt badly that you weren't able to date, I didn't mean Ethan Ames."

Indignation exploded in Sam's stomach. "How is that any different from Mike fawning over you? Isn't he a *paying guest,* too?"

Angie's eyes widened and her arms dropped to her sides in surprise. The motion caught Sam's eye and she gasped at what was obviously missing from her mother's finger—her diamond wedding ring. "Mom, your ring—" Sam's voice choked. No. She couldn't be ready to move on that fast. Panic gripped Sam's heart.

Angie's expression softened, and sympathy filled her eyes. "We should finish this discussion outside."

* * *

Ethan stared at Daniel across the cabin. "I can't believe you told my dad."

Daniel crossed his arms behind his head as he reclined against the bed pillows. "I call it like I see it, man."

Anger burned in Ethan's gut. "You don't know what you saw." Daniel also didn't know what his telling Jeffrey had done. Or did he? Ethan's father would probably be banging on the door any minute. Ethan swallowed, trying to control his temper, when all he wanted to do was leap across the worn bedspread and strangle his cousin. "You just did this because you're jealous. My dad sent you to try to weasel into Sam's life when I didn't give him any info about the property. You can't handle the fact that Sam's not interested in you."

Daniel's eyes flashed and he sat up straight. "That's not how it seemed when we were dancing."

Ethan jerked forward a step, and Daniel held up both hands with a chuckle.

"What do you think you're going to do, cousin? Less than two weeks on a ranch and you're suddenly so tough?" Daniel stood and faced Ethan head-on. "Just because you can stay on a horse and throw some hay bales around doesn't make you a cowboy. Or even a real man, for that matter."

Ethan's fists balled. "And you think womanizing for your own financial gain makes you a real man?"

"You want to hold up a mirror when you say that next time?"

Ethan's mouth opened, then shut.

Daniel smirked. "Exactly. We're cut from the same cloth, cousin. Whether you like it or not."

No. Ethan refused to believe he could be as cold-hearted as Daniel or Jeffrey. He truly cared about Sam, on a level deeper than Daniel's attraction to her physical appearance alone—if he was even truly attracted. Knowing Daniel, it was only the lure of the chase that appealed. Sam definitely wasn't Daniel's typical target for romance. If Ethan had been able to hide his feelings for Sam from Daniel longer, his cousin might not have seen her as a challenge. He'd learned Daniel's competitive nature over the years—an attribute in business, but a coffin nail in personal relationships. Ethan took a steadying breath. "Look, I don't want to fight."

"No, you don't." Daniel swaggered forward. "I can guarantee that."

Ethan glared back. How could he ever have considered Daniel a friend? Had Ethan's own morals ever been low enough that they used to have things in common?

Daniel grabbed his room key off the nightstand. "I'm out of here, man. Good luck with Sam." He laughed coarsely as he headed for the door. "You'll need it." The door slammed behind him with a solid bang.

Ethan stalked into the bathroom and slammed that door, too, just because he could. He bent and rested his forearms against the cool porcelain sink, rubbing his temples with his fingers. This entire project had become impossible. At this point, how could he please anyone? Not Jeffrey, unless Ethan betrayed everything he'd finally found good in himself and destroyed the ranch so Angie would accept their insulting offer. That definitely wasn't an option. But he couldn't please Sam, either, especially if she found out why Ethan was really there and where he worked. No wonder she'd been so adamant against a relationship with him, despite the obvious mutual attraction. It was a miracle they were even friends—and by the time this project was over, Ethan would be lucky if she'd stoop low enough to spit on him while passing him on the street.

Unless he got out of it now.

Ethan slowly lifted his head. What would happen if he just cut his ties with the business and abandoned the company? He could confess everything to Sam, beg for her forgiveness, and help find a way to save her farm. He could be her loan, could arrange some form of payment for Noble Star so Sam could bring back the breeding business without having to ride in the rodeo. He could even find himself a place nearby, and live in a cheap apartment until Sam's farm was back in the black and she felt able to pursue a relationship.

Ethan groaned as reality struck a cold punch. Who was he kidding? Sam would never forgive him for the deceit, even if technically he'd been omitting information about his career, and not lying. But it felt the same to his heart, and it would to hers, too. She'd never forgive him.

Ethan's head throbbed. It was a nasty game of timing, and the clock kept striking louder and louder. He felt seconds from doomsday, one way or another. Please his father, and not be able to live with his own conscience? Or please Sam and be guilt free—but alone and broke? He'd still have his family in the first scenario, but how long until his father's love and respect hinged on another unscrupulous business practice? If the target wasn't Sam and her family, it'd just be some other family, somewhere down the line.

He'd never be free of it.

God, what do I do? His headache pounded again in his temples and Ethan reached to open the mirrored medicine cabinet for an aspirin. His sleeve snagged the same piece of loose paneling from the other day and he ripped his arm away, too frustrated to care if his shirt tore. The paneling cracked and Ethan winced. Now the wood splintered from the wall and stuck out even farther than before. Great, just what he needed—to confess to Sam that he'd torn up the cabin's bathroom.

Ethan tried to press the protruding piece back in place, but it refused to stick. He craned his head and peered around the edge. His eyes widened and he swallowed. He'd been in the real estate industry long enough to recognize the splintered, chipped wood that appeared to spread behind the entire wall.

Termites.

It was chicken to pretend to be sick, but nevertheless, Sam sat on the couch in the living room in the dark, save for the sunlight streaming through the closed miniblinds and the glow of the TV flickering images across the carpet. She adjusted the throw blanket over her shoulders and snuggled into the worn fabric of the sofa. Maybe she wasn't pretending after all. Watching the home videos of her father made her stomach churn and her forehead sweat worse than if she had a fever.

She'd dug the videos from the box in her room, something else Angie had put away with Wade's trophies and awards—and now, her wedding ring. Something must have changed in her mother's heart during the bonfire, and maybe it was good she was able to move on—but that didn't mean Sam had to be happy that men like Mike were hanging around. Mike would never be Dad.

No one would ever be Dad.

The conversation with Angie on the back steps left Sam's heart pierced with guilt. She shouldn't have spouted off at her mother like that, no matter how indignant she'd felt. But the kiss with Ethan had happened so fast. It wasn't as if she'd planned it. Besides, the odds of someone seeing them by the barn were low—though apparently not as low as she'd thought if Daniel was busy spreading the word. At least her mom now understood the kiss was an accident, not something they'd planned.

Imagined, dreamed of, yes. But not planned. Still, the thought of running into Ethan or having another argument with her mother left Sam weak and tired. Watching home movies of her father wasn't exactly going to help, but sometimes, it felt good to wallow.

Sam angled the remote at the TV and lowered the volume. Her father, handsome under a cowboy hat, smiled at the camera, which shook under Angie's unpracticed grip. His drawl sounded thicker than Sam remembered as he lifted a child version of Sam onto a black speckled pony. "Boots go here." He pointed to the stirrups and Sam watched herself nervously correct her position.

"Back straight." Wade winked at the camera. "Now smile, darlin'. This is fun."

Sam grinned as the younger version of herself waved and beamed with missing teeth. "Hi, Mama!"

"Be careful, honey." Angie's tense voice sounded from behind the camera. "Wade, watch her."

"I've got her, honey." Wade took the lead rope on the pony's halter and began to walk away. His voice softened. "I'll always have her."

A moment later, the camera shut off with a tilted view of the ground and a beep. Sam clutched the remote with both hands, eyes glued to the white-and-black static scratching across the screen. Her heart cracked again for the hundredth time since her father's death and she didn't try to stop the tear that rolled from the corner of her eye.

What was she doing? She couldn't enter the rodeo, couldn't put herself in the same position as her father had brazenly placed himself. What if something went wrong and Angie had to go through the same pain all over again? Sam swallowed, and the remote fell from her fingers onto the floor. She couldn't risk it, not even for the money. She couldn't put a price tag on her life. There'd been one on Wade Jenson's, and it was labeled fame and glory. She refused to die for the same.

She had too much to live for.

Relief flooded Sam's heart in waves, healing the cracked surface and washing away the crevices of fear. She closed her eyes as more tears dripped off her cheeks. She wouldn't enter the rodeo. There had to be another way to find the money she needed for the breeding business, just like her friends had been trying to convince her. God would provide, wouldn't He? Could she trust that, for once?

Ethan's face filled Sam's mind and her eyes opened abruptly. She sat up straight and untangled the blanket from her legs. Her thoughts raced with figures and numbers and she nodded slowly. Ethan—the proverbial spur in her side—might be the answer to her prayers after all.

Chapter Twenty-One

Ethan slipped away from his parents' cabin, the screen door banging in his wake. He quickly scaled the stairs toward the main house, hoping to find Sam. He'd snuck in his parents' suite and with a quick tug of a pry bar he'd borrowed from the barn, confirmed the termite damage was in their cabin, too—which meant the little critters likely resided in all of them. They'd need a professional to tell, but it was an obvious problem that wasn't going away.

His heart sank as he mentally compiled the tally sheet for that level of repair. It'd be costly for Sam and her mother, to put it mildly. Talk about bad timing. Here she was risking her life to earn money at the rodeo and this setback would probably take a huge chunk of the winnings—if she even placed in the event. What if she didn't? How would they get by? If the Jensons' credit cards were already maxed, it was safe to assume any savings were also depleted. Maybe their insurance coverage would be enough—if they'd been able to make their payments in light of their current trouble.

He reached the main house and hesitated at the bottom

step, one hand grasping the warm staircase railing. Sam had to be inside—she hadn't been at the barn or saddling up the horses with Cole for the morning ride. But was Ethan ready to see her? Their kiss still burned in his memory hotter than the sun now coating his back. He couldn't look at Sam and pretend he didn't feel what he felt. Not that it was exactly a secret, after his verbal confession the night before. Still, one rejection was enough—he couldn't take seeing a second one in her eyes.

Ethan took a step forward, and the stair creaked under his weight. Sam had a right to know what was happening to her family's property. This could change everything for the worse for Sam and Angie financially. At best, it would be a giant inconvenience. They'd have to shut the ranch down for weeks if not longer to do the repairs and construction. That'd be loss of income on top of the cost of repairs.

He backed off the step onto the ground, his boots hitting the earth with a thud. Right now, he was the only one who knew about the damage. It'd be a matter of time before it was evident, of course—but if he told Sam and Angie, Jeffrey would find out, as well, when word spread about the ranch temporarily shutting down. It'd be the perfect ammo for his dad to barge in, guns blazing, and convince Angie to sign on the dotted line. Knowing the extent of the damage, Angie would then consider Jeffrey's insultingly low offer a good one, not realizing how little termite damage mattered to a developer with a bulldozer waiting to level the property for a strip mall.

A light in the front window of the house clicked off and Ethan eased away from the house, his heart pounding loudly in his chest. Maybe he should keep quiet about the discovery for now, until his family went back to New York—

hopefully *without* the contract in hand. Then he could call Sam and tell her privately so they could take care of the repairs. There'd be less chance of Jeffrey finding out and ruining things for Sam's family that way. Maybe by then he'd have given up on the property and turned his business sights elsewhere.

Ethan turned and headed toward the barn to try to catch the morning riders before they left for the trail.

Sam clutched her handwritten paper with sweaty palms as she hurried down the porch steps. Hopefully Ethan would be back from the morning ride by now and she could pitch her plan. She hadn't talked to him since their kiss at the barn the night before and he was probably wondering where she was and if she was avoiding him. Awkward as it would be to face Ethan, she had to do it—for the ranch. She pushed aside the other, scarier reason hovering in her heart. It didn't matter what she wanted personally with Ethan. She would enlist his help for the sake of her family, for her father's memory—that was it.

She trudged toward the barn, her boots stirring up the dry Texas dust from the grass. Okay, so maybe it was for more than just the ranch or for her dad's honor. But she'd never been the fairy-tale type growing up. As a girl she was more interested in the horses pulling Cinderella's carriage than the princess doll, but something about Ethan sparked the desire to be rescued. Every girl needed a knight at some point in their life—even if hers drove a silver sports car instead of a silver steed.

Sam couldn't help but grin at the thought of Ethan on a horse in period clothing. Prince or not, he would help her. He obviously had the finances to do so, and if the confession of his feelings last night was true, then he'd want to. Besides, he'd mentioned not too long ago that he would be willing to help her figure something out if she'd just avoid the rodeo. He wouldn't have forgotten the offer—would he?

Her stomach twisted with equal parts nerves and hope, and the paper in her hand bunched under her tight grip. She'd worked out the figures and how much she'd be able to give Ethan back monthly until the debt was paid. It'd take a while, but if the breeding business boomed again as it should, then it would be worth it. Ethan might brush off the offer of repayment, but she couldn't let him. Even if they were dating, she'd insist on returning the money.

Sam paused on her way to the barn. Dating? Yeah, right. But the idea draped over her heart like a cozy, familiar blanket and she took a moment to bask in the inner warmth. Her and Ethan—ridiculous on all accounts. Yet people made long-distance relationships work every day. Who was to say they couldn't give it a try? With Ethan's wealth, he could travel as often as he wanted.

You don't even know what he does for his money. Sam shook her head, the fantasy fading to the back of her mind even as the hope lingered. Attraction or not, love or not, it would never work. They were too different. So why was her heart still pounding at the mere idea? Maybe it was worth at least talking about with him.

Ethan's muffled voice sounded from inside the stables and Sam picked up her pace, eager to see him.

"I can't believe you would keep something that important from me." Jeffrey Ames's voice boomed from inside the shadows of the barn and Sam instinctively stepped away. She peered around the edge of the door frame. Jeffrey's bulky figure and Ethan's trimmer one was just made visible at the other end of the barn, in front of Wildfire's stall. Ethan held a bridle in one hand as if he'd been in the process of untacking the gelding before talking to his father.

"I just found out this morning," Ethan snapped in response, and Sam winced.

Jeffrey's arms crossed over his middle and he seemed to grow even taller. "You could have found me. Daniel did. Don't you know this changes everything?"

Ethan mumbled something Sam couldn't catch and she leaned closer, ears straining.

Jeffrey's head shook. "She's gotten to you, hasn't she?" The words came out more like a statement than a question. Sam eased back around the white frame. Was she the one he referred to? She had to be. Who else had Ethan met while in Appleback? But why did it matter to Ethan's dad?

Jeffrey continued. "You've forgotten why we're here, Ethan. Why *you* are here. Daniel has once again done your job, and done it well. So you can quit the love act with Sam. It's accomplished nothing." He snorted. "I should just give Daniel all the commission from the sale of this ranch, but your mother would never allow it."

Sam recoiled from the door, dread clenching her throat. She sucked in her breath, and the shadows inside the barn darkened until even the sunlight around her seemed dim. Ethan had been pretending to care for her. The friendship, the chores around the farm, the kiss—all of it was to buy her family's ranch.

Ethan started talking, but Jeffrey interrupted him. "You better get your head out of the clouds and start focusing on what's important. Your business is at stake. I didn't make you head of the real estate division of Ames Development for you to slack off."

The earth tilted toward her and Sam braced her weight against the barn wall. Somewhere behind her, a horse nickered, but it sounded as if from a tunnel. That explained why he'd been so secretive about his job. Ethan had used her. She should have known never to trust him. And after she'd confided in him about her father, and the rodeo—no wonder he tried to talk her out of riding! If she won the prize money, the farm wouldn't need to be sold. Surely her mother didn't know what Ethan and his dad were up to. Angie would never keep something like that from her. They were a team.

Regret rose in Sam's heart. It wasn't exactly teamlike of her to keep the secret of the rodeo from her mother. She shoved aside the guilt. Part of her wanted to run to her room and cry, the other part—the survivor part that'd kept her going these years since her dad's death—wanted to storm into the barn and tell Ethan exactly what she thought of him and his manipulative family. Her fists clenched and the carefully prepared finance plan scraped into her palm. The pain jerked her back to reality.

"Dad, listen." Ethan's voice cut through the barn. "Let me explain."

Sam shook her head and she fisted the paper into a ball. Ethan's words weren't directed at her, but it didn't matter. She'd heard plenty. Sam hurled the paper wad at the barn wall as hard as she could and hurried back toward the house, tears blinding her eyes. She wasn't sure what made her the most upset—feeling naive and immature for not seeing the deception coming, or knowing that the ranch might very well be sold out from under her.

She swiped at her tears before throwing open the screen door on the porch. Or maybe the reason for the sob in her throat was because any potential relationship with Ethan was now officially gone.

Chapter Twenty-Two

Ethan slammed his fist into the stall door and winced at the splinters that scraped his knuckles. He kicked the door then leaned forward, resting his palms against the rough wood. His dad left, finally—but not before giving Ethan an earful. How much longer could Ethan put up with this nonsense? He was a grown man, but as long as he stayed under his father's roof—proverbially and literally—he'd never break the vicious cycle of lies and manipulation.

Ethan straightened. Enough was enough. Sam deserved the truth, and he would tell her. He was through with the deception, regardless of the consequences to his checking account, business résumé—and love life. If he had to move clear across the country to find work, so be it—and this time it'd be a career that he wanted for himself, not a job he'd been pressured into by his controlling parents. Too bad the only thing Ethan could picture himself doing was right here in the middle of Texas—about as far from his level of expertise as he could get. But every rancher started out somewhere, didn't they?

As for his love life, well, he'd never win Sam's heart by keeping the truth from her. She might forgive him if he spoke up now. The longer he waited, the faster that door would slam shut and lock.

Footsteps sounded behind him and Ethan turned. Sam strolled across the hay-strewn floor toward him, angry red blotches spotting her neck and cheeks.

"Sam? Are you okay?" He held out his hand toward her but let it fall to his side at her violent glare.

"How dare you?" Her hands shook at her sides and she folded them tightly across her chest. "I heard your conversation with your father."

Ethan's heart landed somewhere near their booted feet. "Sam, let me explain."

"No." She poked his chest with her finger, and he automatically dodged her next attempt. "I'll do the talking. That way you can't lie anymore."

"I never meant to—"

"Deceive me? Manipulate me? Kiss me?" Sam scoffed. "I confided in you, Ethan. I told you about my dad, my dreams for this ranch, my fears of losing it." She squeezed her eyes shut before shooting him another fiery dart of hate. "Fears that have been your goal all along."

Ethan cringed. She was right, but not in the way she thought. "No, Samantha, that's not entirely true. I—"

"Don't call me that." Her voice, low and controlled, shook with audible restraint. "Don't ever call me that again." She poked him harder. "And why don't you take your offer to buy this farm and shove it inside your shiny little sports car on your way back to New York. Because I can assure you, my mother will never sell this place."

"Sam, there's really something you should know." Ethan grabbed her hand and held on, but she wrenched it free of his grasp.

"I know all I need to." Sam turned and strode toward the barn entrance, then paused. "I know I shouldn't have ever trusted you." Her figure, silhouetted by the sun, vanished as she stalked outside into the light.

Ethan collapsed against the stall door and sighed. Wildfire nickered and Ethan rubbed the horse's shaggy neck. "I'm too late, boy. She's made up her mind." Wildfire snorted and Ethan shook his head. "You should know better than me once Sam gets something in her head, that's it." He rubbed his watering eyes and drew a shaky breath. Time to pick up the pieces. It wouldn't be the first time, and unless he left his father's business, it definitely wouldn't be the last.

"I'll be seeing you." Ethan patted Wildfire's nose, then brushed his hands on his jeans as he made his way down the barn aisle.

Sam pulled the ranch truck into Kate's driveway and yanked the key from the ignition. Somehow, Sam had managed to make it through the rest of her chores and avoid Ethan. Not that it'd been all that hard. He'd probably gone back to his cabin to mope—and hopefully pack. She shoved away the pang that accompanied thoughts of Ethan leaving. It'd all been a lie. How could she miss that? Yet the memories refused to let her go.

She climbed from the cab and headed toward the front door. Kate met her on the porch with a sympathetic smile. "You okay? You sounded pretty upset on the phone."

"I will be." Sam lifted her chin and inhaled deeply. "As long as you made more brownies."

"Of course." Kate hesitated in the doorway, then opened her arms. "I think you need a hug more."

Sam allowed Kate's brief embrace, then fell against her

friend with a sob. "I trusted him, Kate. I think—I think I even loved him. And now…" Her voice cracked.

Kate squeezed her harder. "Listen, it wasn't your fault. You had no idea." She drew back and ushered Sam inside. "Have you talked to your mom yet?"

"No, I couldn't find her all day." Sam swiped at her eyes as she headed for the kitchen, following the aroma of chocolate. "She's probably somewhere with that Mike guy again." Her stomach grumbled.

Kate plucked a brownie from the pan and put it on a small saucer for Sam. "Have you really thought about all this?"

Sam shrugged, brownie coating her teeth. She swallowed. "As much as I want to think about my mom dating again."

"Not that." Kate leaned her hip against the counter. "I mean Ethan. Yeah, it looks bad, but don't forget all the good things he did."

Yeah, right. Sam snorted and took another bite.

"Seriously." Kate raised her eyebrows. "All his help around the ranch. The dance you said y'all shared at the party. His natural instincts with the horses. It couldn't all be fake."

"Sure it could." But doubt pierced Sam's conviction, and the brownie suddenly tasted like dust. Had she been too hasty in judging Ethan? He had been adamantly trying to tell her something in the barn, but in her anger she'd ranted and raved and never gave him a chance. The brownie settled like a stone in her stomach and she dropped the remaining bit on her plate.

"Uh-huh." Kate crossed her arms. "Whatever you're thinking, keep heading down that path. I can tell by your eyes you're considering it."

"Why are you so eager for me to give Ethan a chance, anyway? No one in that family seems to have a single redeeming quality."

"But you and Ethan really shared something." Kate pointed her finger as Sam's mouth opened. "Don't try to deny it. No more lies."

No more lies. Sam briefly closed her eyes. If only Ethan could abide by the same rule. Was it too late? Had she been wrong to verbally attack him that way? Maybe she'd overreacted. Her spine stiffened and Sam shook her head. No, she hadn't overreacted. But she could at least hear Ethan's side. Maybe he did know something she should.

But first, she had to talk to her mom about the sale. She deserved to be warned.

"Thanks for the chocolate—and the advice." Sam smiled at her friend. "There's some people I need to find."

"Go." Kate gently shoved Sam toward the door. "And keep me posted."

"You know I will." She headed back for her truck, her heart lighter even if her stomach felt heavier. The only way to fix this mess was the truth—the entire truth, even to her mother about the rodeo.

Sam cranked the key in the starter and backed out of Kate's driveway. No more lies.

Ethan shoved open the cabin door, noted the empty room and slammed it. He couldn't find his parents or Daniel—not a good sign. It was early evening, and he'd skipped dinner to avoid Sam and to get a head start on his packing. He'd figured his parents would be around after the meal, but he'd already checked their cabin, the entertainment lodge and the barn. Somehow Ethan had to stop his family from offering Angie a low price because of the termite damage. She deserved the truth, just as Sam did. The news was financially devastating, but it didn't merit the underhanded deal his father was sure to try and get away with. If Angie would just take the time to do the proper research, maybe call in some favors from locals, they might be able to swing it—especially with Sam's contribution from the rodeo winnings.

He stepped outside onto the porch, desperate to escape both his thoughts of Sam and the proximity of the open suitcase on his bed. Ethan had to leave, knew this day was coming two weeks ago, but he didn't think it'd be under these negative terms.

Yeah, right. Did you think Sam would give you a going-away party with cake and balloons after you ripped out her heart? Ethan's conscience mocked him. He squeezed the porch railing. He was lying to himself now. Maybe the Ames family manipulation gene was too far buried in his DNA. Maybe it was hopeless to even try to be different. *God, do I even stand a chance?* The breeze rocking the branches of a nearby tree was his only answer.

Across the field, the front door of the main house opened and Jeffrey Ames descended the rickety porch steps, pausing at the bottom to shake Angie Jenson's hand with a big smile. Ethan sucked in his breath, noting the bundle of papers in both his dad's grip and Angie's.

He was too late.

Chapter Twenty-Three

Sam quickly threw on her jeans and the nearest T-shirt by her bed. She couldn't believe she'd slept through her alarm, and on the same morning she wanted to try to find Ethan before starting the morning chores. She wrestled her feet into her boots, hoping it wasn't too late. After leaving Kate's house yesterday afternoon, she'd unsuccessfully tried to hunt down her mother to confess her rodeo plans. Former rodeo plans, anyway—though unless she worked out a deal with Ethan, Sam was financially back at square one.

But Angie had remained MIA and it wasn't until nearly dinnertime Sam remembered her mom said she'd be going into town for the day to talk to a few local banks. Sam had tried Ethan's cabin next, but he and Daniel had been out—or more likely—Ethan was still avoiding her. And rightly so, after the way she'd railroaded him. Sam still wasn't sure how they'd get past this bump in their developing relationship—no, make that a giant pothole—but the love gasping in her cracked heart demanded she try.

Even if it was impossible.

Sam thundered down the stairs into the kitchen. Clara looked up from baking, her usual bright smile absent.

"What's wrong?" Sam's stomach pitched and she paused at the foot of the steps.

Clara motioned her head toward an envelope lying on the table. "Jeffrey Ames left this here over an hour ago. Said it was for your mother." She turned back to her dough but peeked at Sam over her shoulder. "I could tell from the bold print through the envelope what was inside. I'm sorry."

Sam trudged toward the thick white envelope lying on the wooden surface, and plucked a thick stack of papers from inside. She picked up the handwritten note with a shaky hand.

Ms. Jenson,
Business matters insisted we return to New York at once. Please find the attached check for our stay. Everything was just as you described it. I'm sorry the recent termite discovery changed our initial offer on your property, but rest assured you are still making the right decision. Please sign and return these sale papers at your earliest convenience.
Sincerely,
Jeffrey Ames
Ames Family Real Estate

Sam's heart skipped, then thudded twice against her chest. Initial offer? Her mother knew who the Ames were this whole time—and accepted a bid to buy the ranch? Sam grabbed the papers, the bold word *CONTRACT* taunting her from the first page. Her hands trembled and she dropped the papers back on the table as if they might burn her skin. Betrayed by the man she loved and her own flesh-and-blood mother. Who else was keeping secrets from her? And what termite damage existed on the ranch? Her world rocked on its axis and Sam steadied herself against the table.

"Again, I'm so sorry." Clara's soft voice punctured the thin wall temporarily damming Sam's emotions.

Sam stifled a cry with her hand. "I've got to go." She grabbed the truck keys from the hook and raced out the back door, her mind a spinning blur. Her mom didn't have enough faith in them to get through this tough time financially, didn't believe Sam when she told her it would work out, and now, apparently didn't even trust Sam enough to let her help make a decision as important as selling the family farm. All this time Sam thought she and her mother were a team, when in reality, her mom had only seen Sam as a child.

The door slammed behind Sam as she jogged toward the truck. How dare Ethan! He not only kept the truth about his family's occupation and came to the ranch intending to buy it out from Sam, but he knew that Angie was in on the whole thing and never told her. How foolish Sam must have looked, talking about how close she and her mother were and how she wished Ethan could have that same relationship with his father. Now Ethan was gone, and with him the last remnant of hope that they'd shared something special.

Sam jammed the truck into gear and squealed down the driveway, dirt and gravel mixing into a thick cloud that floated through the open window. She coughed. Ethan obviously didn't need her, and she refused to need him. Even if the ache in her heart never went away.

She steered the truck toward town and angrily swiped the dust from her face. She'd show them both. She'd save this farm on her own, starting with officially entering the rodeo. She still had time. She'd practice the rest of the week and hope that Cole's training, her exercises, and own sheer determination would be enough to succeed.

A tear tracked down her cheek and Sam brushed it away with her sleeve. She didn't need her family, or Ethan. Riding for her dad's honor and knowing that she'd finally earned the title of Rodeo Sweetheart for him would be all she needed.

That, and maybe a heart transplant when this was all over.

Ethan hated the stiff shirt collar around his neck, hated the phone ringing incessantly in his office, even hated the gleaming, spotless mahogany desk. But most of all, he hated the sick feeling in his stomach that hadn't budged an inch since leaving Appleback, Texas, a week ago.

He slapped the disconnect button on the telephone and dropped into his rolling chair. Usually the supple leather was a comfort, but today the smell only reminded him of the tack at Jenson Farms—soon to be yet another strip mall—and the horses he'd left behind. Who ever thought Ethan Ames, corporate real estate executive to a competitive firm, would miss an animal? Especially one that was three times his size and stank more often than not?

The only thing hurting Ethan's stomach worse than the new hobbies he'd abandoned was imagining Sam's face when she found the letter his father left with the cook, Clara—and the accompanying paperwork.

"Ethan." Daniel stepped inside Ethan's office, his hands plunged into the crisp pockets of his navy suit. "You gotta snap out of it, man. I told you I was sorry for scooping you with your dad."

"Scooping me?" Ethan stared in disbelief. "You think I'm upset because you told my father about the termites first?"

Daniel shrugged.

"You don't get it. You never have."

"I'm sorry!"

"I know. But that doesn't change anything, does it?" Ethan stood, refusing to give Daniel even an inch of ground. "Innocent people still got hurt. A family ranch still will turn into a mall, and the woman I love—" His voice faltered.

Daniel's eyebrows shot up. "Love? I had no idea it was so serious."

"That's because you never think of anything but your own motivations."

Daniel rocked back on his heels, his brow furrowed.

"Just forget it, okay? It's too late." Ethan rubbed his temples with his fingers, turning his back on his cousin. He didn't particularly want to see the view of the city from his office window, hated the reminder of how much he had and how little Sam did—but it was better than looking at Daniel any longer.

"It's not too late." The whoosh of the air conditioner clicking on almost drowned out Daniel's soft response.

Ethan crossed his arms, his back still turned, eyes focused on the city bustling beneath their high-rise building. "Yes, it is. The deal is done and Sam will never forgive me." *I'll never forgive myself.*

"It's not done until Angie mails her signed paperwork in." Daniel's footsteps shuffled across the thick carpet and Ethan's back straightened at the truth in his cousin's words. "It's not too late—if you can get to Appleback and convince Angie why she shouldn't take the offer after all."

Ethan spun around, grabbing Daniel's arms with both hands. "Why would you even suggest this? You already have my dad's favor and the corner office." His eyes narrowed. "What else is left to take? You've won."

Daniel stared back into Ethan's eyes. "I don't blame you for not trusting me. I've jerked you around as much as anyone else has in this business." His gaze flickered over Ethan's shoulder, then back. "But you're different, man. You don't want any of this. This isn't your world anymore." He offered a little shrug. "So why don't you go back and save the world you do want?"

Ethan's heart blasted his chest in full force, and he shook Daniel slightly. His cousin might be unpredictable and not the trustworthiest, but he did have a point—a great point. "Do I have your word you won't tell my father?"

Daniel checked his watch. "You've got a four-hour head start. Some of us still have to do what it takes to make it in this business, and that means not suffering the wrath of Jeffrey Ames."

Ethan clapped his cousin's shoulder and abruptly released him. He'd take what he could get. He reached over and grabbed his leather briefcase from under his desk and hurried for the door. Daniel remained in the center of the room, and Ethan paused briefly in the frame. "Thanks, cuz."

Daniel grinned. "Go get 'em, cowboy."

Ethan left the office before Daniel could change his mind. But three steps down the plush hall, he knew there was one more step he had to take—in the opposite direction from the elevator. He turned on his heel and pushed open the heavy glass door to his father's office.

Jeffrey Ames looked up with a start from his desk. "Ever heard of knocking?"

Ethan crossed his arms over his pounding heart. "I'm leaving."

"Fine. Bring me a coffee when you get back. And see if Daniel wants anything." Jeffrey continued marking on paperwork with his pen. "Make mine nonfat this time."

"No, Dad. You don't understand. I'm leaving the company—for good." Ethan widened his stance, prepared for the verbal blows about to fly.

Jeffrey's pen lowered and he finally looked up. "What's that?"

"I'm done, Dad. Enough is enough. Let's be honest—I'm not what you want for this company, and believe me, this company isn't what I want."

Jeffrey stood, his imposing figure seemingly towering above Ethan even though their height difference was only an inch or two. Ethan lifted his chin, refusing to back down. This decision should have been made months ago, maybe even longer, and he would stand his ground.

Even if his knees shook a little.

"Are you insulting my life's work?" A growl formed in the back of Jeffrey's throat.

"I won't, though trust me, it's not from lack of material." Ethan shoved his hands in his pockets, hoping the move made him look more casual than he felt. "Daniel is better suited for this job, Dad. Always has been, and you've never had a problem pointing that out. So don't even pretend to be upset. You replaced me a long time ago."

Jeffrey harrumphed as he settled back into his chair. "That may be, but what do you think you're going to do? With no money or prospects—"

"I've got money."

Jeffrey's eyebrows bunched but he remained silent.

"I've been preparing for this day, and it's here. So, I'll be in touch." Or not. Ethan would make that call later. After Jeffrey found out what Ethan was truly leaving to do in Appleback, he'd probably be denied access to his family for a long time. As much as that thought stung, it was the only choice. Ethan refused to sacrifice his morals, ethics and character for his shady father one more time. God would provide for Ethan, would surely bless his obedience for doing the right thing.

And if Ethan still struggled financially, well, then at least he would be on the same page with Sam.

"I won't stop you." Jeffrey shrugged, picking up his pen once again. "Good luck with whatever you choose to attempt. You'll need it."

Yet another dig at his capabilities, but this time, the barb didn't pierce as deep. *Thank you, God.* Ethan gave his father a brief nod before striding down the hall to the elevator, peace making his steps lighter—until grim reality settled on his shoulders. He'd just walked away from the only security he'd ever known, and a future with Sam was iffy at best.

But like it or not, Sam's prince was riding in to save the day. Ethan checked the time on his cell phone as the elevator doors opened with a ding, and grimaced.

Even if he might be a little late.

Chapter Twenty-Four

The arena buzzed with the sound of excited chatter, stomping hooves, and cracking lariats. Horses snorted and bulls pawed the ground, cloaking the worn bleachers and fence rails with a fine layer of dust. Sam clapped her hands against her leather chaps, more of a nervous release than an attempt to rid them of dirt.

"Don't worry, Sam, you look great." Kate smiled. "And you're going to do great."

"Thanks." Sam tried to return it but the effort made her nauseous. Too bad her appearance couldn't be her top concern of the moment. She shook out her hands, wishing the adrenaline had a release from her tense body.

"You okay, kid?" Cole gripped Sam's shoulder with one hand, his eyes boring into hers. "You don't have to do this."

"If you know me at all, then you already know my response to that." Sam adjusted the white paper number on the front of her vest. Seven—her dad's number. Hopefully the number would apply to her father's successful career instead of his tragic last ride. She gulped. No point in thinking of that right now. She had a job to do—distractions would only get her hurt.

Or worse.

"All right, then." Cole squeezed Sam's arm and turned her toward the chutes. "Go line up. They'll be calling your number in a bit."

"I'm going to get some lemonade. You want a drink before you ride?" Kate gestured toward the snack booth set up on the far side of the bleachers.

Sam shook her head. "No, thanks. My stomach can't handle it." She managed a slight wave at Kate before turning to join the line of riders—all male. She straightened to her full height, refusing to let them intimidate her. Sam was competing against them, yes, but more than that—she was competing against herself. Her throbbing left shoulder testified to that, as did her sore back and tight quad muscles. She resisted the urge to rub the cramp forming in her calf. Maybe practicing the majority of the night on Lucy wasn't the best idea. Then again, a full night's sleep wasn't much ammo against the thousand-plus pound animal in the chute, either.

The bull nearest Sam huffed, and the fluorescent arena lights glinted off the giant ring in his nose. Sudden panic gripped Sam in a vise and she clutched Cole's sleeve with both hands. "Am I crazy?"

Cole pried his shirt from her grip. "You just said you made your decision. So quit acting like a greenhorn."

"I know." Sam swallowed. "But it's a crazy decision."

"An inexperienced female bull rider competing in the same rodeo her father used to? Nothing but crazy." Cole's voice softened. "But you can do it. You're ready."

"I practiced on a steer, Cole. A *steer.*" Sam's voice trembled and she couldn't tear her gaze away from the bulls waiting their turn—for revenge. She shook her head to clear it. "4-H kids ride steers. Those giant animals in those chutes are the real deal. I might as well have been practicing on a dairy cow."

"That's not true, and you know it. Quit spurring on your fear." Cole shoved his cowboy hat away from his eyes and held Sam's gaze. "The same concepts apply to both steer and bull riding. Grip with your legs, keep your upper body loose, and counterbalance by leaning the opposite direction of the buck." He tapped the top of Sam's hat. "The rest is up here."

Sam nodded slowly. She could do this. She *would* do this—for her dad. Her mother might not believe in her, but Sam would prove her wrong. She'd avoided Angie the majority of the week, throwing herself into her chores and her training. Sam couldn't look at her mom without the fury of the secret sale boiling in her stomach—right beside the guilt of her own kept secrets she tried to ignore.

She'd prove Ethan wrong, too. Just remembering his betrayal sent a spark of anger trailing Sam's spine. It also made her heart pound painfully in her chest, but she wouldn't think about that right now. The love still residing within would catch up to her mind's resolve soon enough. In the meantime, there were bigger issues to conquer. Her eyes narrowed. "I'm ready."

She had to win. Losing would only earn Sam a permanent job at the dude ranch and the title of laughingstock among the male competitors—not to mention a likely ride in an ambulance. She forced back a shudder. *Focus, focus.*

"Up next, number thirteen, George Daniels." The announcer's drawl boomed over the loudspeaker with a burst of static. "On deck, contestants number four and seven."

"That's you." Cole nudged Sam toward the chutes. "Eyes on the target, kid. You can do it. I'll be there in a few to help you mount."

Sam's boots—and previous burst of self confidence—felt

connected to someone else as she shuffled her way toward the line of riders. *God, help me. I don't want to make the same mistake Dad did.*

Ethan thrust a handful of bills into the taxi driver's hand and jumped from the cab. There'd been no time to arrange a car rental from the airport. He slammed the door and raced up the walk to the main house. *Please let them be inside, please let them be inside.* The prayer echoed in rhythm to his pounding heart as he banged on the front door. He waited, then knocked again.

Clara opened the door, a spatula in one hand and a firm wrinkle nestled between her drawn eyebrows. "Can I help you?" Attitude radiated from her apron-covered body and Ethan took a step back.

"I'm looking for Samantha—I mean, Sam, and Angie. Are they here?" He craned his head to look over Clara's shoulder, but she pulled the door halfway shut.

"I believe that's none of your concern." Her arms crossed over her chest and Ethan took another step away.

"It's important. Please." He heard the panic in his voice and cleared his throat. "I can't let her— It's urgent. Trust me."

"Can't let her what?" Clara's hand holding the spatula lowered and the frown on her face eased.

Ethan ran a hand over his hair and huffed an impatient breath. "I can't let her sell the ranch to my father's company."

"Your father's company? I thought it was yours, too."

"Not since I left a few hours ago to come warn Angie and Sam about his intentions."

Clara's lips twitched to the side. "Well, why didn't you say so in the first place? You better stop her quick. Angie signed the papers and just left for the post office to mail them. Never seen a body so discouraged. But she was taking 'em anyway."

"She's already gone? Where's the post office?" Ethan's hands balled into fists. He couldn't have come this far to be too late. Maybe he could fly back to the office in New York and catch the letters in the mail before they reached his father—assuming he would even be allowed back on the premises after this move he pulled.

"You can still catch Ms. Jenson. The post office is only a mile or two away. Take one of the horses." Clara pointed to the barn. "Looks like Wildfire is still saddled from the afternoon ride. I know Cole won't mind if you borrow him, he's not here anyway."

Ethan stopped on his trek down the stairs. "Where is he?" Cole never left the ranch except for supplies, not even when he was sick last weekend.

Clara glanced over her shoulder, then back down at Ethan. "You didn't hear this from me, but Cole and Sam are at some rodeo in town. I don't know what they're up to, but I know they have secrets. Big ones."

Ethan's heart jumpstarted with a jerk. The rodeo. That was tonight? His head swam and he gripped the staircase railing. Sam was going to ride—and he wouldn't be there. What if she got hurt? He squeezed his eyes shut as panic racked his senses.

He couldn't be in two places at once. Stop Angie from mailing the contract, or stop Sam from making a huge—and potentially deadly—mistake?

Sam's breath came in tight gasps. The cowboy on her right nudged her with his shoulder. "You okay there?"

She forced a smile and squeezed the rail with both hands. The dirt ground under her feet felt as sure as quicksand. "Fine." *Just perfect. I'm about to die the same way my father did.* Terror gripped her with two hands and she struggled against the panic clawing at her lungs.

"Good luck." The cowboy, number four, tipped his hat to her and moved up in line to take his turn.

Sam couldn't help but stare as he easily scaled the chute and settled on the bull's broad back. He made it look so easy. She squeezed her eyes shut. *You can do this, you can do this. Oh, no I can't!* Was the farm worth it? Worth her life? If she died, there would be no breeding business to enjoy again. No more horseback riding. No more campfires and trail rides and long talks with Kate.

No more kisses with Ethan.

Her heart skipped a beat and Sam opened her eyes. Dust flew as a bell dinged and cowboy number four charged into the arena. She stared unseeing as a dozen memories with Ethan flickered before her. His taut arm muscles as he lifted bale after bale of hay into the bed of her truck. The expression of content he wore while ambling beside her on a trail ride. His dark chocolate gaze daring her to hate him. Oh, how she'd tried. But Ethan's true character overcame the prejudiced, city-slicker label she'd stuck on him at his arrival, and he quickly became a real cowboy in her eyes.

If he hadn't betrayed her, she'd have easily entertained ideas of him being the one.

A buzzer sounded and jerked Sam from her thoughts. She swallowed as contestant number four slipped from the bull and jogged to the chute. The horned beast galloped toward the clown attendants waiting for him, and they quickly corralled the animal at the other end of the arena.

She was next. It would take several minutes to ready the next bull, so she had five, eight minutes tops to stall.

Or escape.

Sam rubbed slick palms down her jeans. *Just breathe.* She inhaled deeply but the anxiety refused to let go. *God, if I'm making a mistake, stop me!*

"Sam!"

Sam's eyes widened at the familiar voice calling to her from the stands. She turned just in time to see Ethan and her mother running to her through the crowd, pushing past a man in a black hat and nearly knocking over a young girl with braided pigtails.

Ethan reached Sam first, grabbing her shoulders with both hands. He panted, trying to catch his breath. "You can't—please don't—" He squeezed her arms and tried again. "Don't hate me."

Tears crowded Sam's eyes and she blinked rapidly against the threatening torrent. "Why not?" Her heart screamed a thousand reasons why not and she begged them to shut up. Ethan had betrayed her, had kissed her as if he meant it and pretended to like her. To love her. All for the sake of a real estate sale.

But could he really have pretended that realistically?

"Why not?" Ethan's voice pleaded over the sudden applause from the stands behind them. "Because I'm here." His eyes searched hers and Sam turned away. But her hands shook for reasons completely outside her pending bull ride, and she couldn't deny it another minute. She opened her mouth, still unsure what to say, but her mom interrupted.

"Sam, don't do this." Angie brushed messy hair from her eyes and futilely tried to push the loose strands into her ponytail. "I should have told you about Jeffrey's offer. But I wanted to make the best decision for us, and knew that you would influence me toward keeping the property. Sometimes you're too strong for your own good. I wanted you to be able to get on with your life." She let out her breath. "But I had no idea how much the breeding farm really meant to you until Ethan talked to me on the way here."

"What choice do we have? If I don't ride, you're going to sell." Sam's voice caught in her throat and a few of the tears pressing against her lids slipped free. "You might still sell anyway."

"No, she's not. Or rather, she shouldn't." Ethan reached toward Sam, then let his hand fall to his side. Her fingers burned just imagining the contact and she squeezed her hand into a protective fist. Ethan continued, turning to Angie. "My dad can't be trusted. The highway is being relocated near your ranch. If he buys your property, it's being turned into a strip mall. He lied about his intentions in order to offer a lower price. I've known that, but thought if I could just play his game long enough, I could escape it all. But there's no escaping his level of lying and manipulation." He exhaled slowly. "I just thought if I held in there a little longer and stayed on the inside, I could protect you, Sam. I'm sorry for deceiving you. I never meant to."

"I know." The words left her lips before she could fully process and Sam blinked in surprise.

"You do?" Ethan's head dipped toward hers.

She nodded and wiped at her eyes. "I do." The truth filled her heart in sweet relief. She knew Ethan couldn't hurt her that badly, not after all they'd been through together. The doubts scratched the surface but deep down, Sam knew better. The overheard conversation and anger at Angie over selling the ranch had pushed Sam over the edge. If she'd just thought long enough about Ethan's true character, the man he'd been slowly revealing himself to be these past couple weeks, she would have seen it was a mistake.

Ethan reached again for Sam's hand. And slowly, carefully, she threaded her fingers through his.

Chapter Twenty-Five

Ethan's heart raced at the gentle contact with Sam. He swallowed against the knot rising in his throat. "Do you forgive me? I did lie to you—at first because I was doing my job. But then to protect you. But I'm done, Sam. No more manipulation. No more false pretenses. It's just me." His hands shook and he squeezed her fingers, hoping she couldn't feel the desperation in his touch. "Hopefully that's enough."

"Oh, I think it's plenty." Sam smiled up at him and his stomach pitched like he was riding a roller coaster—or maybe a bull. Her lips parted slightly and he automatically leaned closer.

Angie cleared her throat. Sam winced. "Sorry, Mom."

"You don't have to apologize." Angie gestured toward the arena. "But I believe they just called your number. Your dad's number." Her eyes darkened with emotion.

Sam shook her head at Angie's drawn expression. "I can't do this to you, Mom. I thought I could, but I can't. It's not worth it. Even if we lose the farm."

Angie crossed her arms. "I don't want to accept Mr. Ames's

offer, especially if he's turning our beloved property into a mall. But with this termite issue, I'm not sure how the ranch will survive otherwise."

"Unless I ride." Sam's eyes shut briefly and she sighed.

"I have an alternative plan." Ethan tugged at Sam's hand to get her attention. His next statement would either seal their relationship or ruin it for good. But he had to try. He couldn't stand by and let the Jenson farm go to ruins when he had the means to stop it. "Look, I'm buying Noble Star for your ranch, and that's that. You can think of it as a business investment or pay me back however and whenever you want, but I'm doing it." *Or maybe you'll marry me in the next six months and the stallion will become mine along with your heart.* He smiled, hoping Sam couldn't read his eyes. Too soon for the M word—but not for long.

Sam's mouth opened and Ethan gently tapped her chin to close it. "And that's that."

"Ethan, I can't let you do this." Angie touched Ethan's shoulder, stepping closer as a family carrying popcorn shouldered past them toward the stadium seats. "It's too much."

"You don't realize all you two have done for me." Ethan slipped his arm around Sam's waist, glad the pressing crowd gave him reason to lean closer to speak. "You Jenson women showed me how a family is supposed to operate. Without that inspiration, I might never have gotten the guts to quit my father's business and try life on my own. So consider this my gift back to you." The purchase would negatively affect his savings account, but at the moment, he could think of no worthier cause. He'd figure it out—get a real job or even two. Whatever it took.

Angie's eyes filled with tears and she nodded slowly. "I can do that. Sam, can you?"

Ethan tucked a lock of Sam's hair behind her ear and she studied his expression before nodding slowly. "I think so. But we *will* pay you back."

His heart swelled with the reality of what she was entrusting him with, and he smiled in relief. But there was a catch. "I wasn't finished." He cupped Sam's chin in his hand and held her gaze. "I want you to ride."

"What?" Sam's eyes widened. "I thought that was the whole point of your offer—to keep me from riding. It's all you've wanted since you got here—for various reasons." She rolled her eyes.

"The main reason was because I was worried about you." Ethan drew his hand from her face. "But I know you, Sam. If you don't do everything in your power to meet your goals, you'll never be happy—and you'll end up resenting me for buying Noble Star, even if you pay me back. You'll always wonder what if."

"And what if I win?" Her eyebrows quirked into a question mark.

"Then the prize money will go to the ranch and the cost of repairs for the termites and whatever else you need." Ethan gestured toward the arena and the bulls waiting in the chutes. "It's your choice. I support you regardless."

"But, Mom…" Sam's voice trailed off and she cast an anxious expression at Angie. "I can't. You'd never forgive me."

"If it's important to you, then do it." Angie's voice, soft and firm, barely rose about the noise of the spectators and announcer.

"Are you sure?" Sam's cheeks flushed.

"Make your father proud, honey. He'd want this." Angie turned Sam toward the chutes. "You've worked so hard to get here. If you want to do this, we'll be in the stands cheering you on."

Sam stumbled toward the pen, looking over her shoulder only once before giving a determined nod. Her gaze lingered on Ethan, then with shoulders shoved back, she marched toward the bulls.

Angie gripped Ethan's arm with white knuckles. "I hope I'm not making a mistake."

Sam really hoped she wasn't making a mistake. She quickly made her way toward the pen, half hoping she was too late and her call was over. But the other cowboys by the pen motioned for her to hurry.

"Just in time." Cole appeared to her right and guided her to the chute. He hoisted her onto the fence. "Where've you been?"

She swung one leg over the rail. "Ethan and Mom are here."

Cole's lips twisted. "Good. But don't get distracted." He gave her a final boost.

Sam gasped as she settled on the bull's wide, leathery haunches. *Too fast, too fast.* She couldn't catch her breath, couldn't think. Couldn't process. Her legs gripped both sides of the bull automatically and Cole helped her wind her hand around the rope.

"Hang on tight." He cinched the cord tighter. "How's that feel?"

Sam wiggled her gloved fingers beneath the rope. "Secure." Right. Like there was anything secure about what she was going to do.

A cowboy hanging on the fence nearby squinted at Sam beneath his hat. "You ever done this before?"

Sam managed to shake her head once before two other riders to her left laughed. "Good luck, darlin'." One nudged his friend with his elbow and shook his head.

"Shut it or beat it." Cole gave the group a menacing glare

and they quickly snapped their mouths closed and looked the other direction.

"And now, contestant number seven, Samantha Jenson." The announcer's drawl rang through the arena and a hush blanketed the crowd. Sam sucked in her breath. She must have accidentally scrawled her full name on the sign-up form. Now the entire arena knew she was the only female contestant of the night. Could she really pull this off?

"Focus." Cole's voice brought her back to the present, away from memories of her dad and away from Ethan and Angie sitting exactly six rows up in the bleachers.

"Looks like we've got a potential Rodeo Sweetheart here tonight." The announcer chuckled. "Good luck, honey!"

"Why does everyone keep saying that?" Sam gritted her teeth.

Cole flashed a white smile and dropped backward off the fence. "Good luck." He tipped his hat at her and nodded to the chute attendants.

The buzzer sounded, the gate opened, and Sam bit back a scream. She squeezed with both legs until her leg muscles felt numb. The bull rocked forward, wild and out of control. Sam struggled to keep her eyes open. She tried to focus on the giant beast's head, so she could predict which way to lean. *Just like on Lucy.* No, who she was kidding? This bull was bigger, meaner, and faster—not to mention more likely to chase her when she fell off. Sam forced the thought from her mind. *Hang on, hang on.*

The seconds ticked by but felt like months. Dirt stirred by the bull's hooves slapped her face. Her body ached but adrenaline drowned out the cry of her muscles. Somewhere behind her, Cole's voice rang through the noise and cries of the spectators, and she focused on his encouragement. Then Ethan's cry rose above the crowd. "You can do it, Sam!" She clung to his words as she twisted left, then right.

"Two seconds left!"

Sam wasn't sure who yelled those inspiring words but she clenched her teeth and found a deeper level of strength. Two seconds. She could do this. Not for her dad, not for the ranch, but for herself.

The bull gave a final buck just as the buzzer sounded. Sam's arm dropped like a limp noodle from her death grip on the rope and she slipped from the animal's broad back. *Run, run!* But she collapsed to the ground, her legs unable to support her, as the bull pounded the earth. Dirt crowded her vision and she coughed, curling into a protective ball. A flash of red and yellow to her left proved the rodeo clowns were doing their job, and within seconds the bull was at the other end of the arena.

Sam struggled to her knees. *It's over, it's over.* The chant echoed in her mind but all she could hear was the roar of the spectators, on their feet and applauding. Cole jogged to her side and helped her stand. "Samantha! Samantha!" The crowd cheered and stamped in rhythm.

Tears pressed Sam's eyes as she smiled at Ethan, who was clapping so hard she thought he might sprain his arm. Tears poured down her mom's face, and matching ones slipped down Sam's cheeks as Ethan, Kate and Angie began making their way down the bleachers toward the arena. She'd done it. But there was one last thing to do.

She tugged off her dusty cowboy hat and threw it high above her head. It spiraled into the air in a blurry, tan arch. *This one's for you, Dad.*

Ethan met her at the side of the pen. Sam scooped up her

discarded hat before climbing over to join him. She dropped into his arms. He squeezed her in a tight embrace and then stepped back to meet her gaze. "You were amazing."

"I was terrified." Sam laughed and her throat felt raw. She'd done it. Now it was a matter of waiting for her score. But she was already a winner—even if it felt at the moment she had spaghetti noodles for arms.

Ethan's hands rested on her waist and she forgot the ache in her muscles. "By the way, did I tell you I was leaving the real estate business?"

Sam shrugged. "I sort of figured that when you said you left your father's company to come warn us about him."

"Well, I forgot to mention there's one more sale I still have to make."

Sam frowned. "What do you mean?"

"You know that vacant property down the street from Kate? One hundred acres, small catfish pond, three-bedroom ranch house?"

Sam nodded. "It's been for sale for months."

"Not for very much longer." Ethan grinned.

Sam's eyes widened. "You mean—"

Ethan cut her off with a kiss, which she gladly returned. She wound her arms around his neck and breathed in his spicy cologne.

Angie and Kate joined them by the pen, and Sam reluctantly ended the kiss. Angie looped her arm around Sam's shoulders and squeezed. "They're about to announce the winners." The relief dripping from her voice nestled in Sam's heart and she hugged her mother back. It was over. No matter what happened from here, they were going to be okay.

"You did so good!" Kate squealed and joined the group hug around Sam. "Just don't do that again anytime soon, okay? I think I was just as nervous as you were." She clutched her stomach.

Cole stepped up beside them, and elbowed Sam's ribs. "It's in the bag, kid. That bull was mean."

"Now you tell me." But even sarcasm couldn't dampen the joy bubbling in Sam's heart. The farm still needed the money, but even if Sam didn't place, she'd found what she was looking for. Peace. Contentment. Happiness.

And Ethan. She looked up at him and smiled, then realized she'd been tuning out the announcer.

"Contestant number thirteen, George Daniels, eighty-nine out of a possible one hundred points."

Sam winced. That was a great score. Her nails dug into Ethan's shirtsleeve and Angie's arm tightened around Sam.

"Dennis Montgomery, contestant four, seventy-two!"

Cole sucked in his breath. "You should be next."

The announcer paused as papers shuffled over the loudspeaker. "And finally, contestant number seven, Samantha Jenson, with a score of eighty-eight. Congratulations to our winner, George!"

"Second place!" Cole ruffled Sam's hair. "Not bad, kid. There's a cash prize for that."

"Sam, I can't believe it." Angie grabbed her into a hug. "Your father would be so proud! I'm so proud."

Sam hugged her, then pulled back. "I want the farm to have all the money." She reached over and took Ethan's hand. "Use it for whatever we need the most, Mom. If we need to keep running the dude ranch, it's fine by me."

"Are you sure?" A puzzled frown tightened Angie's brows. "But the breeding business—"

"Sam, it's your dream." Kate's head tilted to one side. "It's what you've worked for this whole time."

"I'm sure. If it hadn't been for our family's new venture into dude ranching, I've have never met Ethan." Sam grinned at Cole. "But if you do keep the dude ranch, you have to hire Cole some extra help." She winked and Cole laughed.

Angie nodded. "We'll figure out all the details later. With your prize winnings, we have options now." She brushed a tear from Sam's cheek. "Go get your check, baby. We'll meet you at the truck." She motioned for Cole and Kate to follow her, leaving Sam alone with Ethan—or as alone as they could be in a crowded arena.

"I'm so proud of you, Samantha." He winced. "I'm sorry, I've got to quit calling you that."

"No, I want you to." She reached up and touched his cheek. "At first I was riding for money. Then for my dad. But I realized something while I was out there on that bull. Mainly, that I was crazy." She shuddered and laughed. "But secondly, that this was for me all along. I needed to make peace with the past. Mom finally moved on from Dad's death. But I couldn't do that without proving to myself what I was capable of."

He smoothed her hair. "You're the strongest woman I know."

"I realize now that being strong outwardly wasn't being strong emotionally. Like my mom said, sometimes I'm so strong that I live in denial. I had to accept my dad's death—not drive myself crazy trying to prove myself to him or to his memory. I finally feel like I've made him proud. Not because I rode a bull, but because I realized it's okay to move on, to live like he would have wanted me to." She smiled. "So call me Samantha. I think my dad would like that."

"I can do that." Ethan wrapped his arms around Sam and she snuggled against him with a sigh. "Exhausting day."

"No kidding." She laughed hoarsely.

"Looks like you didn't win the title of Rodeo Sweetheart after all."

"Titles are overrated." Sam mumbled into his shirt, inhaling the crisp aroma of laundry detergent mixed with the familiar scent of horses and leather.

"You'll always be my sweetheart," Ethan whispered into her hair, and she shivered.

"Promise?"

"Isn't a real cowboy as good as his word?" Ethan smiled.

Sam grinned back. "I don't see a real cowboy around here."

Ethan stiffened in protest. "Hey, I've made some real progress—"

"You didn't let me finish."

He quirked an eyebrow.

Sam tightened her grip around him and rose up on tiptoe to meet him face-to-face. "I only see the one man capable of lassoing my heart." She pressed her lips against his before Ethan could argue.

But from the way he kissed her back, she knew he wouldn't have anyway.

* * * * *

Dear Reader,

Like most girls, I went through a horse-crazy phase that never really went away. After begging God for a horse of my own for years, you can imagine how ecstatic I was when my parents finally granted my wish in junior high. I became the proud owner of a paint horse named Bo, and although we had to sell Bo when I got into high school, I still carry sweet memories of him to this day. So when I first got a glimpse of Sam's story, I grew excited, eager to dive back into my horse-crazy roots and paint my readers a word-picture on a Texas ranch.

In June 2009, while writing this novel, my husband and daughter and I took a trip to see my mother-in-law in south Louisiana. I told my husband I wanted to take a picture of me on one of her quarter horses, thinking it'd be a cute way to promote this book later.

Well, I got my picture, but I don't think it'll ever be printed. About thirty minutes after I took the picture and rode for a bit, my mother-in-law mounted the same horse and had a traumatic accident. She was in a coma for months and as of today, we're still not sure what level of brain activity or physical function she'll ever get back.

This book was hard to write. Not just because of the deadlines I faced during times of family crisis, but because I was hurt. I was scared. I was mad. I didn't know if I wanted to even think about horses, much less write about them. But I kept on, and with God's help and the encouragement of my friends, I did it. And I'm glad. Because I know for a fact that if my mother-in-law was physically able to today, she'd get right back on the horse she'd fallen from.

So this is my tribute to her.

Many blessings,

Betsy St. Amant

QUESTIONS FOR DISCUSSION

1. Sam's family ranch is everything to her. Have you ever been particularly attached to a house or piece of land before? Why?

2. One of the reasons Sam is so anxious to make her family home what it used to be is because of her father. Have you ever tried to do something in honor of a lost loved one? What was it?

3. In the story, Sam feels that she can't talk openly with her mother Angie about her plans to bull ride because she feels her mom would disagree and talk her out of her goal. Have you ever had to keep a secret in order to do what you felt was the right thing?

4. When Sam first met Ethan, she labeled him a "city slicker" and a "greenhorn tourist." Have you ever judged someone prematurely before meeting them? Why?

5. Ethan was immediately attracted to Sam because she was so different from the type of girls he was used to seeing in New York. Do you believe opposites attract as a rule or as an exception?

6. Ethan's family was at the ranch under false pretences. After Ethan got to know Sam, he wanted to share his secret with her. Why did he feel he couldn't yet?

7. Jeffrey Ames only cared about wealth and status, even at the sacrifice of his own son. Do you know anyone

who has allowed the greed of the world to overcome them in this way? How do you handle being around such people?

8. Sam and Ethan were an unlikely match—seemingly polar opposites. But what did Sam and Ethan have in common?

9. Sam was willing to put her very life on the line in a dangerous attempt to meet her goals. Have you ever been so passionate about something that you risked your life to succeed? How did the situation turn out? Would you do it again?

10. Sam's best friend, Kate, was a stable force in Sam's chaotic life. What friends have you had over the years that were there for you in a crisis?

11. In the story, Sam rode a mechanical bull at the town fair. Have you ever ridden a mechanical bull? What was your experience like?

12. Sam is very comfortable around horses, having spent her entire life on them and around them. Do you enjoy horseback riding? When was the first time you ever rode a horse?

13. Ethan was willing to put the comfort of his wealthy lifestyle aside when he fell in love with Sam. Have you ever had to change careers or lifestyles in order to be with your spouse or significant other?

14. When Ethan revealed his father's plans for the Jenson ranch, Sam knew she had misinterpreted Ethan's inten-

tions. Have you ever been in a misunderstanding with someone that hurt you, only to find out you had misunderstood them? How did you get past the hurt?

15. When Sam rides in the rodeo at the end, she tosses her hat in a tribute to her father. Have you ever made a public gesture in honor of a loved one in your life? Tell us about it.

Here's a sneak peek at
THE WEDDING GARDEN
by Linda Goodnight,
the second book in her new miniseries
REDEMPTION RIVER,
available in May 2010 from Love Inspired.

One step into the living room and she froze again, pan aloft.

A hulking shape stood in shadow just inside the French doors leading out to the garden veranda. This was not Pop-bottle Jones. This was a big, bulky, dangerous-looking man. She raised the pan higher.

"What do you want?"

"Annie?" He stepped into the light.

All the blood drained from Annie's face. Her mouth went as dry as saltines. "Sloan Hawkins?"

The man removed a pair of silver aviator sunglasses and hung them on the neck of his black rock-and-roll T-shirt. He'd rolled the sleeves up, baring muscular biceps. A pair of eyes too blue to define narrowed, looking her over as though he were a wolf and she a bunny rabbit.

Annie suppressed an annoying shiver.

It was Sloan, all right, though older and with more muscle. His nearly black hair was shorter now—no more bad-boy curl over the forehead—but bad boy screamed off him in waves just the same. He was devastatingly handsome, in a tough, rugged, manly kind of way. The years had been kind to Sloan Hawkins.

She really wanted to hate him, but she'd already wasted too much emotion on this outlaw. With God's help she'd learned to forgive. But she wasn't about to forget.

Will Sloan and Annie's faith be strong
enough to see them through
the pain of the past and allow them to open
their hearts to a possible future?
Find out in THE WEDDING GARDEN
by Linda Goodnight,
available May 2010 from Love Inspired.

TITLES AVAILABLE NEXT MONTH

Available April 27, 2010

THE WEDDING GARDEN
Redemption River
Linda Goodnight

WIFE WANTED IN DRY CREEK
Janet Tronstad

HOMETOWN PRINCESS
Lenora Worth

A DAUGHTER'S LEGACY
Virginia Smith

THE MARRIAGE MISSION
Pam Andrews

THE ROAD TO FORGIVENESS
Leigh Bale

LICNMBPA0410